The Praise of Shakespeare
An English Anthology

Sir Sidney Lee and C. E. Hughes

Alpha Editions

This edition published in 2024

ISBN 9789361473814

Design and Setting By

Alpha Editions

www.alphaedis.com

Email - info@alphaedis.com

Contents

PREFACE

I BELIEVE this volume serves a useful purpose. It is the fruit of a suggestion which I made to its compiler, Mr. Hughes, in the following circumstances.

At the beginning of last year I engaged in controversy in the *Times* newspaper with certain persons who laboured under the delusion that the evidence of Shakespeare's authorship of those plays and poems, which for three centuries have been published as his, was inconclusive. In defiance of the fact that the acknowledged work of Bacon, the prose writer and philosopher, proves him to be incapable of writing verse of genuine merit, some of my opponents held Bacon and no other to be responsible for those manifestations of supreme poetic genius which are associated with Shakespeare's name. Other sceptics, of less raw judgment, hesitated to commit themselves to this extravagance,—they confined themselves to the slightly more plausible contention that the facts recorded of Shakespeare by contemporaries were scanty, and that his career was clothed in a mystery, which justified wild attempts at a solution.

The whole of the sceptical argument ignored alike the results of recent Shakespearean research and the elementary truths of Elizabethan literary history. But confirmed sceptics are not easily convinced of defects of knowledge. With especial emphasis did even the most enlightened among those who declared their doubt in print, persist in affirming that Shakespeare was unnoticed by his contemporaries, and that his achievements failed to win reputation in his lifetime or in the generations succeeding his death. It was that allegation, to a greater degree than any other, which seemed to encourage the inference that the received tradition of the Shakespearean authorship of the plays needed revision.

The conjecture that Shakespeare lived and died unhonoured rests on no foundation of fact. The converse alone is true. Shakespeare's eminence was fully acknowledged by his contemporaries, and their acknowledgments have long been familiar to scholars.

Yet the reiterated assertion that Shakespeare's contemporaries left on record no recognition of his worth, proved that information on the subject was narrowly diffused, and that public intelligence suffered by the strait limits as yet assigned to the distribution of genuine knowledge of the topic. I suggested to Mr. Hughes that he should remedy this defect by collecting in a volume that might be generally accessible all notices of Shakespeare which were penned in early days.

Subsequently, when I considered the scheme in detail, I deemed it wise for Mr. Hughes to enlarge its scope so that the volume might form a contribution to the history of opinion respecting Shakespeare of no single period, but of all periods from the earliest to the present day. Thereby the force and persistence of that Shakespearean tradition which ignorance had lately impugned might be rendered plainer, and the liability to misconception might be to a greater degree diminished. The fulfilment of the design on the extended scale might also, I thought, give the work some value as a chart of æsthetic development through the ages. Students of Shakespeare who in the course of three centuries have recorded their impressions of him, include men and women of varying degrees of intellectual capacity, and the orderly presentation of their views could not fail to illustrate with some graphic force the working of the law of taste in literature.

A further justification for the compilation of the work on an exhaustive scale, lies in the fact that it has not been done already. Charles Knight seems to be the only writer who has hitherto attempted any sketch of a general history of opinion respecting Shakespeare. His essay formed part of his *Studies of Shakespeare*, which were first published in 1849, and it was reissued separately as the first volume of a new edition of his Cabinet Edition of *Shakespeare* which was published in London by William S. Orr & Co., of Paternoster Row, in 1851.[vii:1] Knight surveys his subject somewhat perfunctorily from Edmund Spenser to Coleridge. He devotes much space to the eighteenth century, but he pays scant attention to the nineteenth, and he is far from exhaustive in his treatment of earlier periods. Commendable as is his pioneer effort, it is now, alike in form and matter, largely out of date.

A more imposing endeavour was made later to deal with the earlier section of the topic. Dr. Ingleby, a Shakespearean scholar of repute, issued in 1874 the work entitled *Shakespeare's Centurie of Prayse*, in which he dealt with the period extending from the year 1591, when Shakespeare first came into notice as a dramatist, until 1693. A second edition of Dr. Ingleby's volume, revised and enlarged by Miss Toulmin Smith, appeared five years later under the auspices of the New Shakspere Society. A very substantial supplement to this volume, called *Some 300 Fresh Allusions to Shakspere from 1594 to 1694*, was edited by Dr. Furnivall for the New Shakspere Society in 1886. Thus the *Centurie of Prayse* in its final shape extends to 912 pages in quarto. The large book is not at everybody's disposal, but its contents, as far as they go, are very valuable, and no Shakespeare library is complete without it. None the less, it covers less than a third part of that field which a full history of opinion about Shakespeare ought to occupy; it leaves ample room for a treatise on the whole subject.

The general impression produced by Mr. Hughes's extended survey seems creditable to the discernment of the English literary public—of all generations since Shakespeare began to write. The repute that Shakespeare acquired in his lifetime, though it was rarely defined with subtlety, was in spirit all that judicious admirers could desire. The contemporary estimate was authoritatively summed up in the epitaph which was inscribed on his monument in Stratford-on-Avon church soon after his death. In that inscription he was hailed as the equal of great heroes of classical antiquity— of Nestor in wisdom, of Socrates in genius, of Virgil in literary art; he was acknowledged in plain terms to be the greatest of contemporary writers; all living writers were declared to be worthy only to serve him as pages or menials. Shakespeare's epitaph, the significance of which is not always appreciated, justifies no doubt of the supremacy that he enjoyed in the English world of letters of his own day. The homage of literary contemporaries was confirmed without faltering and in finer phrase by Milton, the next occupant of the throne of English letters.

No subsequent change of literary taste or literary fashion in England really dimmed Shakespeare's fame. In the days of the Restoration, Dryden humbly acknowledged discipleship to him. Some censure he suffered from thoughtless lips; but the right to the rank of a classic, which had been granted him as soon as the breath left his body, was never effectually disputed. The formal critics of the eighteenth century sought to show that much of his work deviated from formal standards or from rules of formal art. But these censors gave him the worship of incessant study. They edited and annotated his writings, with the result that a succeeding generation of readers acquired a more accurate comprehension of his work than was possible before. The triumphal progress of Shakespeare's reputation was stimulated by eighteenth century research and criticism to a quicker pace.

The critical faculty of the nation was especially acute and sagacious at the opening of the nineteenth century, and Shakespeare's pre-eminence was then seen in sharper outline and in fuller grandeur than at any earlier epoch. The sympathetic intuition of three early nineteenth century critics—Coleridge, Lamb, and Hazlitt—remains unsurpassed. But there has been no trace of retrogression in the wise and reasoned enthusiasm of later generations of the reading public.

The history of Shakespeare's fame is indeed that of a flowing tide; the ebbing was never long enough sustained to give it genuine importance; the forward march was never seriously impeded, and is from start to finish the commanding feature of the chronicle. If Mr. Hughes's endeavour succeed in impressing that pregnant fact on the public mind, a perilous source of popular misconception regarding Shakespeare's true place in English literary history will be removed.

SIDNEY LEE.

SOME NOTES ON SHAKESPEARE'S REPUTATION

I
INTRODUCTORY

THIS book provides a chronological sequence of the best pieces in verse and prose which the best writers in successive periods have written in praise of Shakespeare, and thereby aims at presenting, as it were, an index to the standard of estimation in which Shakespeare has been held at any given point of time. Thus, as an anthology, it differs in various respects from other anthologies. An anthology, as a rule, hopes to confine itself to pieces of literature intrinsically valuable. The conscientious compiler of an ordinary anthology includes nothing which, according to his own canons of taste, can be considered of doubtful merit. His choice may not always be approved by others—it frequently is not; but he, at least, is satisfied. Here, however, is a different case. My object has been to collect what may be called materials for a history of opinion of Shakespeare, so that as many years as might be of the three centuries and more, which have elapsed since Shakespeare's reputation was born, had to be represented. With these conditions it has not always been possible to exclude bad pieces, for the obvious reason that there has been at times a dearth of good writers. In such cases the best has been given that could be found. The best has at times been deplorably mediocre, but the scheme was inexorable.

The labour of selection has been guided by one or two principles. In the first place, complete poems, or extracts in verse and prose, which relate solely to Shakespeare have been taken in preference to those which mention him in company with his contemporaries. Secondly, passages that exhibit unusual characteristics, whether good or bad, have frequently been chosen. For some of the poor pieces, and I hope they are not many, something may be said. Though their writers are practically forgotten to-day, they were considered great during their own lives; so their productions have at least a historical value. If, then, this volume includes, as I think it does, the best things that have been written about Shakespeare, it includes also many things that in a comparative estimate of the whole must be considered as second-rate, though they happened to be the best in the period during which they were produced. The distinctiveness of the book may perhaps be indicated in this way. An ordinary anthology may be said to gather into a garland the choicest flowers from various fields of literature; this anthology claims to be little more than a collection of botanical specimens.

II
DIVISION INTO PERIODS

The history of opinion of Shakespeare may be divided into three periods, represented broadly by the seventeenth, eighteenth, and nineteenth centuries. Definite limits cannot be assigned to these three periods. Epochs of literary history must be determined ultimately, not by the work produced in them, or by the lives of the producers, but by the influences which gradually brought them into being. Thus, there must always be at the beginning and end of a period of literary history a kind of dovetailing with it of the periods before and after. Still, the three periods I have indicated are reasonably distinct. The first begins with the earliest mention of Shakespeare in print, and may be taken to end with the death of Dryden. The second period was largely affected by Dryden's influence, and thus may be said to begin with the eighteenth century. And the last period, which is due to the reaction from the Augustan age of English literature, may be fairly dated from the beginning of the nineteenth century. The style of the literary products of these three centuries respectively goes to confirm the division. The first period is that of personal knowledge and oral tradition, and tributes to Shakespeare are for the most part in verse. It is the period during which his historical position was in the making. The second period is that of critics and emendators—the period when people begin to realise that there is some great power in Shakespeare's work which finds no parallel in their own time, and must therefore be praised blindly, accounted for, or explained away. Tribute is clothed equally in verse and prose; it is, in short, the period of doubt and astonishment. The last period is that of æsthetic criticism, and tribute is mostly in prose. Shakespeare's position is an accepted fact.

Of the three periods, the second is by far the most interesting to the literary historian. Opinion of Shakespeare during the first period was to a large extent prejudiced by personal knowledge and tradition. The praise is practically equivalent to that of friends; which is to say, it is largely that of blind admiration. In the third period it is open-eyed, intelligent admiration. The matter has been sifted. The question of Shakespeare's genius is no longer a debatable point. The praise is that of disciples who appreciate the logical basis of their master's teaching, and who see the necessity of lucid explanation for the purpose of adding recruits to their number. But the second period is the time of trial. Shakespeare's title to fame is weighed judicially, and is not found wanting.

III
THE FIRST PERIOD

Of the seventeenth century not much need be said, and, indeed, not much that is new can be said. The labours of the New Shakspere Society have added several valuable volumes to the literature relating to Shakespeare's reputation during that period. Of these the *Centurie of Prayse* (of which the second and much enlarged edition was produced under the direction of Miss L. Toulmin Smith in 1879) brought together a very large number of allusions to Shakespeare both in print and manuscript, and these were supplemented by *Some 300 Fresh Allusions*, a work which was edited by Dr. Furnivall in 1886. These volumes display an amazing amount of diligent research, and few additions can be made to their contents. Seven hitherto unnoticed allusions to Shakespeare were discovered by Dr. Edward J. L. Scott in the Sloane Manuscripts at the British Museum, and communicated by him to the *Athenæum* on 5th March 1898.[5:1] This evidence of Shakespeare's reputation during the period under discussion has been ably supplemented by an article entitled *Shakespeare in Oral Tradition*, which Mr. Sidney Lee contributed to the *Nineteenth Century* in January 1902. This traces the actual recollection of Shakespeare by his friends and their descendants, from his personal acquaintance among the actors and the townsfolk of Stratford-on-Avon, to the reminiscences transmitted by word of mouth from Betterton to Nicholas Rowe, the poet's first biographer. Mr. Lee's paper is of the utmost importance. As he points out, "It was obviously the free circulation of the fame of Shakespeare's work which stimulated the activity of interest in his private fortunes, and led to the chronicling of the oral tradition regarding them. It could easily be shown that outside the circle of professional poets, dramatists, actors, and fellow-townsmen, Shakespeare's name was, from his first coming into public notice, constantly on the lips of scholars, statesmen, and men of fashion who had any glimmer of literary taste."

The ground, therefore, may be said to be covered in so far as positive evidence of Shakespeare's fame in the seventeenth century is concerned. But at least three popular fallacies have come into being, and it will be perhaps worth while to state them and definitely refute them. Their existence is due partly to lack of acquaintance with documentary evidence, and partly to misconception.

One of these popular fallacies is that Shakespeare practically vanished from the minds of his countrymen when he retired from the stage; and that what reputation he had in his lifetime was due to his prominence as an actor, rather than to his genius as a poet.

The preface of the First Folio (1623) is enough to prove that this was not the case. The tone of the address "to the great variety of readers" is not that of publishers trying to awaken interest in a forgotten personage, by calling attention to works that used to be popular. The language is that of affectionate friends, the references to Shakespeare those of intimate associates whose memories have not healed of the wound inflicted by his death. It was addressed to the public, not with the diffidence that is born of anxiety lest the subject of eulogy should meet with an indifferent welcome, but with the confidence that is inspired by friendship with a great man who is recognised as a great man.

The second impression of the Folio appeared in 1632, and the spirit of enthusiasm that breathes through the preliminary matter—the publisher's preface and the various sets of verses—has become in no way weakened. The volume contains, indeed, two of the finest poems of direct personal eulogy that have ever been written—that signed I. M. S., and attributed by Coleridge somewhat fancifully to no less a person than John Milton, and the noble *Epitaph on the admirable Dramatic Poet, W. Shakespeare*, actually written by Milton in 1630. No sign of decayed reputation here. Nor elsewhere. King Charles I., it is well known, read Shakespeare. Copies of his plays and poems are mentioned in Prince Rupert's library catalogue. His works were given on the stage, and formed topics of everyday discussion. One might multiply examples of his popularity, but it is striking at shadows.

Another popular error has tinged the traditional notion of Milton's attitude to Shakespeare. It is supposed that his opinion of Shakespeare underwent a complete change from that exhibited in the lines mentioned above. The error that attributes to Milton this surprising revulsion of feeling is due to a misconception of a certain passage in his *Eikonoklastes*. Milton wrote thus:

"Andronicus Comnenus, the Byzantine emperor, though a most cruel tyrant, is reported by Nicetas to have been a most constant reader of Saint Paul's Epistles; and by continual study had so incorporated the phrase and style of that transcendent apostle into all his familiar letters, that the imitation seemed to vie with the original. Yet this availed not to deceive the people of that empire, who, notwithstanding his saint's vizard, tore him to pieces for his tyranny. From stories of this nature, both ancient and modern, which abound, the poets also, and some English, have been in this point so mindful of decorum as to put never more pious words in the mouth of any person than of a tyrant. I shall not instance an abstruse author, wherein the king might be less conversant, but one whom we well know was the closet companion of these his solitudes, William Shakespeare, who introduces the person of Richard the Third, speaking in as high a strain of piety and mortification as is uttered in any passage of this book [*i.e.* the *Eikon Basilike*], and sometimes to the same sense and purpose with some words in this place: 'I intended,' saith he, 'not only to oblige to my friends, but my enemies.' The like saith Richard, Act II. Scene i.:

> "'I do not know that Englishman alive
>
> With whom my soul is any jot at odds,
>
> More than the infant that is born to-night:
>
> I thank my God for my humility.'

Other stuff of this sort may be read throughout the whole tragedy, wherein the poet used not much licence in departing from the truth of history, which delivers him a deep dissembler, not of his affections only, but of religion."

The blundering interpretation of this passage, which Warton accepted and transmitted to his successors, including De Quincey, is that Charles I. was reproved by Milton for having made Shakespeare his closet companion. "The Prince of Wales (afterwards Charles I.)," says De Quincey in his *Life of Shakespeare*, "had learned to appreciate Shakespeare, not originally from reading him, but from witnessing the Court representations of his plays at Whitehall. Afterwards we know that he made Shakespeare his closet companion, for he was reproached with doing so by Milton." A careful perusal of the passage will show that nothing was farther from Milton's intention. Such a deduction is logically impossible. Three things, however, undoubtedly may be deduced from it; and they not only bear a significance directly opposed to the erroneous interpretation, but they are of the highest importance as positive evidence of Milton's appreciation of Shakespeare, and of Shakespeare's literary fame. One may deduce, firstly, that Shakespeare was known, at any rate by name, to the Puritans, who chiefly composed the public for which Milton was writing. Secondly (since Charles was not, we may believe, the man to read in private books that he did not like), that the king's knowledge of Shakespeare was intimate and his appreciation sincere. And, thirdly, that Shakespeare was, in Milton's opinion, one who depicts human nature with accuracy. For, consider the force of the parallel. Milton wrote to show that the deeds of monarchs are not always the substantiation of their words. The Byzantine tyrant, with his mouth full of piety, is cited as one instance; Shakespeare's Richard III. as being, by familiarity, likely to bring the matter home to Charles, is cited as another. Which is, in effect, that Shakespeare's portrayal of a king of such character is, in Milton's opinion, proof that such a king may exist. There is nothing slighting about that. It is high praise.

Milton wrote his *Eikonoklastes* in 1649, when he was forty-one. In 1645 he had written his *L'Allegro*, with the lines:

> "Then to the well-trod stage anon
>
> If Jonson's learned sock be on,
>
> Or sweetest Shakespeare fancy's child,
>
> Warble his native woodnotes wild."

The lines attributed to him in the Second Folio had appeared in 1632, and his fully authenticated *Epitaph* in 1630. Further, his influence has been traced in the notice of Shakespeare which appeared in the *Theatrum Poetarum*, published in 1675 by Edward Phillips, Milton's nephew. Here, surely, is sufficient evidence that throughout his life Milton's early enthusiasm for Shakespeare did not diminish.

A third popular fallacy is that which maintains Shakespeare's reputation to have been at its lowest ebb after the Restoration. This belief is well expressed in Victor Hugo's *Shakespeare*.

"Shakespeare," says Victor Hugo, "once dead entered into oblivion. Under the Restoration he 'completed his eclipse.' He was so thoroughly dead that Davenant, possibly his son, recomposed his pieces. There was no longer any *Macbeth* but the *Macbeth* of Davenant. Dryden speaks of Shakespeare on one occasion in order to say that he is 'out of date.' Lord Shaftesbury calls him 'a wit out of fashion' . . .

"These two men having condemned Shakespeare, the oracle had spoken. England, a country more obedient to conventional opinion than is generally believed, forgot Shakespeare. Some purchaser pulled down his house, New Place. A Rev. Dr. Gastrell cut down and burnt his mulberry-tree.[10:1] At the commencement of the eighteenth century the eclipse was total. In 1707 one called Nahum Tate published a *King Lear*, warning his readers 'that he had borrowed the idea of it from a play which he had read by chance, the work of some nameless author.' This 'nameless author' was Shakespeare."

Now the numerous adaptations of Shakespeare's plays which appeared after the Restoration have been taken somewhat paradoxically as indicative of his decline in the public estimation. Such a deduction is by no means accurate. If we take into consideration the comparatively low level to which imaginative literature had fallen under the influence of Charles II.'s Court, the wonder is perhaps that the theatre-going public should have received Shakespeare in any form. Such neglect of Shakespeare as is seen at this time is attributable merely to change of fashion in popular literature, and that was then, and still is, as mutable as the sea. Popular literature does not live, and the adaptations of the later Stuart reigns are now known only to curious students. But Shakespeare lived through it all, known and appreciated by all who had souls above the vulgar; and in this very period he passed triumphantly his first examination at the hands of a skilled critic, John Dryden. Dryden was in every respect typical of the cultivated class of his period. His early judgment of Shakespeare was formed in the somewhat flickering light of Restoration taste. His final estimate was that of a matured thinker. Certainly, adaptations prepared to suit the fickle taste of the playgoer of the period cannot be said to reflect the true character of Shakespeare's reputation. We see the same thing at the present day. The altruism of theatrical managers is compelled to make concessions to popular demands. The public are still rather shy of going to see Shakespeare simply as Shakespeare. They appear to feel that going to see a play of Shakespeare is like sacrificing themselves for their own good. So the managers who gild the pill for them are successful, and those who do not merely fail, or at best earn a precarious livelihood. One might as well say that Shakespeare's reputation is at a very low ebb to-day, as make the deduction from the fact of the Restoration adaptations. The playgoers of that period wanted something piquant. One may suppose—to put the matter in modern terms—that Heine and De Maupassant collaborating might have produced a popular success. Wycherley and Congreve met the demand as nearly as possible. But Shakespeare was not the thing.

IV
THE SECOND PERIOD

I have taken 1700, the date of Dryden's death, as that which most fittingly marks the close of the first period and the beginning of the second, for it is very soon after that year that the spirit of the eighteenth century begins to make itself manifest. In the history of literature the eighteenth century stands out distinct as a whole. The literature of the seventeenth century had many characteristics, which, even in the most cursory survey, require attention, and these characteristics were mainly due to the connection of literature with the Court. The pedantic James I. was a patron of learning. His son Charles I., and grandson Charles II., inherited the taste for polite letters, and encouraged or influenced indirectly the authors of their times. But the eighteenth century monarchs were different. They did not concern themselves much with men of letters, and literature went its course comparatively unaffected by fashion. But it was affected by the spirit of the age—the spirit born of gradual recognition of the Renaissance. As David Lloyd in his *State Worthies* said of the early seventeenth century, "it was the very guise at that time to be learned; the wits of it were so excellent, the helps and assistants of it were so great; printing was so common; the world (by navigation) so open; great experiments so disclosed; the leisure of men so much, the age so peaceable; and His Majesty, after whom all writ, so knowing." At that time learning was a novelty, and consequently it was fashionable—it was "the very guise." By the eighteenth century great men had grown accustomed to it; and it was becoming the property of the lesser worthies, who, unable to resist the temptation to "show off," turned out reams of didactic verse, the substance of which would nowadays hide its light beneath the respectable bushel of the journal of some scientific society. Dryden was perhaps mainly responsible. He had pronounced the dictum: "They cannot be good poets who are not accustomed to argue well." At any rate, with the eighteenth century the poetry of argument or logic, as distinct from that of inspiration, came into being, and by far the greater part of the poetry of the hundred years that followed Dryden's death was that of poets who are made rather than poets who are born. The same feeling informs the prose. It is true that the age produced Horace Walpole. But Walpole was a literary trifler, and liked to be thought so, though he was amazingly industrious. The eighteenth century saw much excellent prose, but it is almost always the prose of "will" or "must" rather than that of "can." It comes rather of fertility of reason than of fertility of fancy. Of such stock are commentators born.

One finds, accordingly, that the principal producers of pure literature, whether prose or verse, were also critics, and most of them turned their attention, sooner or later, to Shakespeare. Prominent figures in the history of Shakespearean criticism in the eighteenth century stand Pope and Johnson. Both are classical scholars in an age of pedants; both are among the foremost advocates of rigid adherence to prescribed rules in literary production; both place imagination below intellect in estimation of genius; and both are honoured by their fellows as arbiters and dictators of literary taste. Each of them is inclined to say unkind things about Shakespeare, and hardly dares. Pope is the more generous of the two. "It will be," he says, "but fair to allow that most of our author's faults are less to be ascribed to his wrong judgment as a poet, than to his right judgment as a player." Which is to say, that Shakespeare, poor soul! must needs trim his boat to suit the current of popular opinion; that the greater part of his audience in the theatres consisted of low fellows who had never heard of Aristotle, and must not be troubled with the unities and such matters, which they could not understand. One has but to continue this line of argument to conclude that Pope thought Shakespeare so much a part and product of the age in which he was born, that had he been born, say, in Pope's age, he might (which Heaven forbid!) have been a perfect poet according to Pope's lights—might, in fact, have translated Homer, to supply the sixpenny boxes of second-hand booksellers two centuries later. But Pope certainly thought Shakespeare very great. His greatness was, perhaps, not of quite the right kind in Pope's estimation; but greatness he undoubtedly thought it. As to Shakespeare's want of learning, Pope frankly refused to believe in it. He says very wisely:

"There is certainly a vast difference between *learning* and *languages*. How far he was ignorant of the latter I cannot determine; but 'tis plain he had much reading at least, if they will not call it learning. Nor is it any great matter, if a man has knowledge, whether he has it from one language or from another.... I am inclined to think this opinion proceeded originally from the zeal of the partizans of our author and Ben Jonson, as they endeavoured to exalt the one at the expense of the other. It is ever the nature of parties to be in extremes; and nothing is so probable as that because Ben Jonson had much the more learning, it was said on the one hand that Shakespeare had none at all; and because Shakespeare had much the most wit and fancy, it was reported on the other that Jonson wanted both. Because Shakespeare borrowed nothing, it was said that Ben Jonson borrowed everything. Because Jonson did not write extempore, he was reproached with being a year about every piece; and because Shakespeare wrote with ease and rapidity, they cried, he never once made a blot. Nay, the spirit of opposition ran so high, that whatever those of the one side objected to in the other, was taken at the rebound and turned into praises; as injudiciously as their antagonists before had made them objections."

Pope further attributed many of Shakespeare's errors to the carelessness or ignorance of the first publishers of his works, suggesting that the original copies from which they were printed were no better than the *"prompter's book,* or *piecemeal parts* written out for the use of the actors," who may be supposed to have made numerous small excisions and additions.

Thus Pope says in effect that Shakespeare would have been perfect if the age and conditions in which he lived had allowed him. He sees many beauties in him, but he also sees many defects; and his edition of Shakespeare's works is remarkable chiefly for its omissions of passages which the editor deems unworthy of his author.

Dr. Johnson is by no means so ready metaphorically to grasp Shakespeare by the hand. He follows a procession of editors of more or less ability, and he feels that the time has come for the final settlement of Shakespeare's true position. Rowe, the first editor, hardly realised his responsibilities, and his edition of the plays which appeared in 1709 has few merits from the critic's point of view. Pope, who followed him in 1725, had a reputation for brilliance to sustain, and his preface is remarkable rather for neatness of expression than for critical discernment. Theobald came after Pope, in 1733, with much common sense, which made him the laughing-stock of his successors. The next editor, Sir Thomas Hanmer, intended his edition as a tribute to Shakespeare, and what was lacking in criticism was supplied in good paper and printing. Warburton succeeded with a pompous self-assertiveness that expressed itself in amusing but ineffective paradoxes.

Johnson accordingly had a due sense of what was expected of him. His critical equipment consisted in a knowledge of the classical drama, and his æsthetic judgment was founded on the rules by which he had succeeded in his own poetical ventures. Still, he did his best to assume a strictly unbiassed judicial attitude. He did not, as Macaulay states, take it for granted that "the kind of poetry which flourished in his own time, which he had been accustomed to hear praised from his childhood, and which he had himself written with success, was the best kind of poetry." He tried deliberately to approach Shakespeare as he approached the Cock Lane Ghost. He dealt with him as with some mysterious phenomenon which was attracting public attention, and which admitted of explanation. The result was, perhaps, the best balanced common-sense judgment on record. It contained, on the one hand, the most tremendous indictment of Shakespeare that is ever likely to be written; and, on the other, a triumphant defence, coupled with much enthusiastic eulogy. Here are some of the "faults which," as he puts it, "are sufficient to obscure and overwhelm any other merit":

"He sacrifices virtue to convenience."

"His plots are often so loosely formed that a very slight consideration may improve them."

"In many of his plays the latter part is evidently neglected."

"He had no regard to distinction of time or place."

"In his comic scenes he is seldom very successful when he engages his characters in reciprocations of smartness and contests of sarcasm."

"In tragedy his performance seems constantly to be worse, as his labour is more."

"In narration he affects a disproportionate pomp of diction and a wearisome train of circumlocution, and tells the incident imperfectly in many words, which might have been more plainly delivered in few."

"His declamations or set speeches are commonly cold and weak."

"It is incident to him to be now and then entangled with an unwieldy sentiment, which he cannot well express and will not reject."

"What he does best he soon ceases to do."

"A quibble is to Shakespeare what luminous vapours are to the traveller; he follows it at all adventures."

"He neglects the unities—those laws which have been instituted and established by the joint authority of poets and critics."

Johnson proceeds to defend Shakespeare by an excellent demonstration of the absurdity of the unities, and at the close of it owns himself "almost frighted at his own temerity." Then he follows Pope in finding Shakespeare to be hampered by the age in which he lived. "The English nation, in the time of Shakespeare, was yet struggling to emerge from barbarity." Having to appeal to immature intellects, he was compelled to base his plays on novels and traditions well known to his audience, "for his audience could not have followed him through the intricacies of the drama had they not held the thread of the story in their hands." In reply to Voltaire, who expressed wonder that Shakespeare's extravagances should be endured by a nation which had seen the tragedy of *Cato*, Johnson says that "Addison speaks the language of poets, and Shakespeare of men." He proceeds to deal with Shakespeare's learning, and Shakespeare emerges from the ordeal credited with rather less than the average board-school boy of the present day. Johnson decides at length that "if much of his praise is paid by perception and judgment, much is likewise given by custom and veneration"; and, finally, he sums up his merits in the following fine sentence:—

"It therefore is the praise of Shakespeare, that his drama is the mirror of life; that he who has mazed his imagination, in following the phantoms which other writers raise up before him, may here be cured of his delirious ecstasies, by reading human sentiments in human language; by scenes from which a hermit may estimate the transactions of the world, and a confessor predict the progress of the passions."[19:1]

It is difficult in the face of these pros and cons to determine what Johnson's attitude towards Shakespeare really was. Much of his apparent hostility may, perhaps, be attributed to his instinctive argumentativeness. It was his nature to object. If he were in a loquacious mood, you had but to make a bald statement, and he was upon you with an aggressively persuasive "Why, sir!" And here it may be that he felt irresistibly impelled to combat the universal opinion of Shakespeare's greatness, and that he was hardly sincere in all he wrote. However this may be, it is probable that he left on his readers the impression that the balance of his inclination was against rather than for Shakespeare. The very fact of the judicial attitude would tend to produce such an impression. A judicial attitude towards Shakespeare was not at that period so well understood as to be readily distinguished from unfriendliness. And in estimating the critical attitude of the age towards Shakespeare, it is necessary to bear in mind that Dr. Johnson was a more important person when he lived than he is now. Nothing is gained by speculating what he might have thought. The fact remains that what he wrote carried weight.

Johnson's opinion was not, however, sufficiently weighty to make his preface, as he intended it to be, the last word in Shakespearean criticism. Other editors followed him. Edward Capell brought much serious and laborious scholarship to the task; and his judgments were frequently sound, though his lack of perspicuity in delivering them detracts somewhat from their value. His edition appeared in 1768. Five years later, in 1773, George Steevens revised Johnson's edition, and, bringing to the enterprise an unrivalled knowledge of Elizabethan history and literature, embodied many improvements, which he treated with a humour that was frequently malicious and occasionally obscene. To the second edition (1778) of this work was added much valuable material relating to Shakespeare's biography and the sources of his plots, due to the researches of Edmund Malone, who published an edition of his own in 1790. The well-known "First Variorum" edition appeared in twenty-one volumes in 1803, prepared by Isaac Reed from a 1793 copy of Steevens', containing many manuscript notes. The "Second Variorum" appeared in 1813; and the "Third Variorum," arranged by James Boswell, the son of Johnson's biographer, which appeared in 1821, marks the close of what may be called the eighteenth century period of commentators.

It will be seen, then, that Shakespeare was at this time kept prominently before the eyes of the reading public. He was equally a topic of interest with men of letters who confined themselves to no special branch of literature. The attitude of the eighteenth century essayists toward Shakespeare was essentially one of admiration and respect for his genius. They found fault with his plays, it is true, frequently enough, but almost always apologetically. He was not infrequently held up as a model for modern dramatists to follow. The *Connoisseur*, for example, printed a paper discussing the sources of the *Merchant of Venice*; and while elaborating the fact that the plot was borrowed, insisted on the genius displayed in the use which Shakespeare made of it. The *Guardian*, again, enlarges on the naturalness of Shakespeare's characters—remarkable at a time when poetry was, above all things, rhetorical and artificial.

Let us glance now at the poetical critics. It will be noticed that many of the pieces printed in the body of this book appear under names that are not very familiar, and that the eighteenth century is responsible for the majority of them. In modern anthologies it is not usual to include selections from the works of such poets; nor, indeed, if literary excellence be the compiler's object, is it expedient. They are included here not because their effusions appear to me to reach even a modest standard of merit, but because they were accepted as good poets by their contemporaries and by the literary dictator, Dr. Johnson. Johnson, it is true, disclaimed responsibility for the choice of names represented in his edition of British poets, but the repudiation cannot be considered of much importance. Johnson's name had probably more weight with publishers than that of any other man of his time, and it is hardly likely that his advice in the matter of inclusion or rejection, had he thought it worth while to give it, would have been ignored. So one may feel certain that every name on his list appeared with his approval. The laudatory criticisms embodied in the biographies, which he asserted marked the extent of his commission, prove as much. Take Blackmore, for example, whose *Creation* was included, on Johnson's recommendation, in his edition of the poets. "This poem," he says, "if he had written nothing else, would have transmitted him to posterity among the first favourites of the English Muse." Posterity, on the whole, has not given the Muse's favourite much of a welcome, and Blackmore is one of a number of such chosen ones. But even Johnson might have known better. They had their reputations ready made for them by patrons. It was the age of patrons and extravagant compliment, and Shakespeare in the hands of these small poets took a place similar to that of the gods and goddesses of Greece and Rome. Poetical flatterers of great men permitted him to fill the position of comparative in the scale of eulogy, the object of their praises being the superlative. Just as the writers of light society compliments made envious Venus second to Clorinda or Chloe or Celia, so Shakespeare stood aside to find himself excelled by Addison or Pope or Dryden, or even, on exceptional occasions, by some patron who scarcely did more than pretend to throw off little trifles in verse. Witness the "Lines to Mr. Addison," by William Somervile:

> "In heaven he [Shakespeare] sings; on earth your muse supplies
>
> Th' important loss, and heals our weeping eyes."

Or take these lines by John Hughes, "To Mr. Addison on his Tragedy of *Cato*":

> "Great Shakespeare's ghost, the solemn strain to hear
>
> (Methinks I see the laurel'd shade appear!),
>
> Will hover o'er the scene, and wondering view
>
> His favourite Brutus rival'd thus by you."

If one could suppose this to have been written in an ironic vein, the lines would be satisfactorily pointed; but it is impossible, for Hughes continues:

> "Such Roman greatness in each action shines,
>
> Such Roman eloquence adorns your lines,
>
> That sure the Sibyl's books this year foretold,
>
> And in some mystic leaf was found inroll'd,
>
> Rome, turn thy mournful eyes from Afric's shore,
>
> Nor in her sands thy Cato's tomb explore!
>
> When thrice six hundred times the circling sun
>
> His annual race shall through the zodiac run,
>
> An isle remote his monument shall rear,

And every generous Briton pay a tear."

Or take the following by William Pattison, "To Mr. John Saunders, occasioned by a sight of some of his paintings at Cambridge." It would be difficult to imagine a more incongruous bracketing of names than that in the sixth line. The italics are my own:

> "When Nature, from her unexhausted mine,
>
> Resolves to make some mighty science shine;
>
> Her embryo seeds inform the future birth,
>
> Improve the soul, and animate the earth;
>
> From thence, an Homer, or Apelles rise,
>
> *A Shakespeare, or a Saunders*, strike our eyes,
>
> And, lo! the promis'd wonder charms my view,
>
> The old Apelles rivall'd in the new!"

One might quote pages of such stuff—torrents of heroic couplets—whose very form, apart from their sentiment, show that Shakespeare was deemed rather out of date. But the mention of his name counts for something. It means that all of these poets felt, as Dr. Johnson felt, that though they were not quite in sympathy with the old Elizabethan playwright, he was still some one to be reckoned with. Indeed, every now and then the truth comes out that he was too much for them. William Whitehead, for one, had a full appreciation of him.

> "O for a Shakespeare's pencil, while I trace
>
> In nature's breathing paint, the dreary waste
>
> Of Buxton" . . .

he sighs in *An Hymn to the Nymph of Bristol*; and, for all the bathos of its expression, the admiration is genuine.

William Hamilton wrote *A Soliloquy in Imitation of Hamlet*, a paraphrase of the famous speech, almost as bald as that from which Shakespeare copied his. But the effort is doubtless more of a literary exercise than an attempt at improvement of the original, for Hamilton shows at various points in his works a fairly intimate knowledge and real regard for Shakespeare's genius.

Mallet read his Shakespeare intelligently, as witness his *Edwin and Emma*, a love ballad, with its text taken from *Twelfth Night*. And William Shenstone shows the right spirit in this very passable stanza from *The Schoolmistress*, happily describing a village school:

"Yet nurs'd with skill, what dazzling fruits appear!

Ev'n now sagacious foresight points to show

A little bench of heedless bishops here,

And there a chancellor in embryo,

Or bard sublime, if bard may e'er be so,

As Milton, Shakespeare, names that ne'er shall die!

Though now he crawl along the ground so low,

Nor weeting how the muse shall soar on high,

Wishes, poor starveling elf! his paper kite to fly."

That is well meaning and temperate enough, but some of these writers erred on the side of enthusiasm. The following passage from Robert Lloyd's *Shakespeare, an Epistle to Mr. Garrick*, may be quoted as an example:

"Oh, where's the bard, who at one view

Could look the whole creation through,

Who travers'd all the human heart,

Without recourse to Grecian art?

He scorn'd the modes of imitation,

Of altering, pilfering, and translation;

Nor painted horror, grief, or rage,

From models of a former age;

The bright original he took,

And tore the leaf from nature's book.

'Tis Shakespeare, thus, who stands alone."

It will be noted that this effusion approaches Shakespeare through Garrick; and such is the case with many others that must remain unquoted. The reason is that Garrick occupied, by public consent if not by his own desire, the position of Shakespeare's patron. He took, for instance, a leading part in organising the Shakespeare jubilee at Stratford-on-Avon. Among his enterprises on this occasion was the issue of a volume of tributes to

Shakespeare, containing several poetical pieces by himself, distinguished rather for their enthusiasm than for poetical inspiration. Dr. Johnson opened the book with some light verses, addressed to The Fair in a vein of somewhat elephantine playfulness; and Garrick collected into it a number of extracts from various writers, in verse and prose, in praise of Shakespeare, prefacing the whole with a high-flown effort of his own in heroic couplets, and publishing it in handsome quarto.

In the garden of his house at Hampton, Garrick had a temple dedicated to Shakespeare, and adorned with statuary, of which the chief piece, a fine full-length figure by Roubiliac, is now in the entrance hall of the British Museum. But to do him justice, his efforts, though they carried the manner of the playhouse into private life, were conceived in a spirit of genuine appreciation; and if many of his admirers regarded him almost as the rescuer of Shakespeare from oblivion, he, at any rate, was ready to acknowledge his indebtedness to the dramatist on the presentation of whose characters his well-merited fame rested.

So much for the second period.[26:1] Its literature is like a troubled sea of conflicting opinion, through which the ship of Shakespeare's genius sails, tossed and buffeted by winds fair and foul, from all points of the compass, and emerges triumphant.

V
THE THIRD PERIOD

IN the foregoing brief survey I have endeavoured to indicate in the broadest manner possible the principal forces that affected the opinions concerning Shakespeare held during the eighteenth century—the chief boulders, so to say, round which the current of opinion swirled. No such analysis seems necessary in dealing with the nineteenth century. That is, comparatively speaking, smooth water. The poetic reformation inaugurated by Wordsworth and Coleridge, who published their *Lyrical Ballads* in 1798, practically effaced the classic traditions of the previous hundred years, and prepared a way for the school of æsthetic criticism which set Shakespeare in the place which he now holds.

Æsthetic criticism, of a kind, was not entirely unknown. So far back, for instance, as 1736, an anonymous pamphlet appeared with the title, *Some Remarks on the Tragedy of Hamlet, Prince of Denmark*. The author is an enthusiastic admirer of "the greatest tragic writer that ever lived (except Sophocles and Euripides)," though most of the beauties which he points out would be obvious to a reader of average intelligence, and his expositions lack insight. Such efforts were, in fact, nothing more than academic recreation, and but for their evidence of a right tendency are hardly worthy of mention. In effect they were, of course, immeasurably distant from the work of the æsthetic critics of the early nineteenth century. Coleridge spoke truly when he thus described his achievement:

"However inferior in ability I may be to some who have followed me, I own I am proud that I was the first in time who publicly demonstrated to the full extent of the position, that the supposed irregularity and extravagances of Shakespeare were the mere dreams of a pedantry that arraigned the eagle because it had not the dimensions of the swan."[28:1]

One has but to mention Hazlitt as Coleridge's co-worker to feel that Shakespeare's position can never be seriously called in question.

In the mass of literature, much of it excellent, that has sprung from this beginning, two works only—in English prose—are so pre-eminent as to demand mention here, Mr. Swinburne's *Study of Shakespeare* (1880), and Professor Dowden's *Shakespeare, his Mind and Art* (1874). Of these, Mr. Swinburne's book astounds one with a flow of eulogistic rhetoric that can only be compared with the marvellous piece of inspired enthusiasm on the same subject by Victor Hugo.

In nineteenth century verse Shakespeare's name appears comparatively seldom, excepting in poems written directly in his honour. This is a logical result of the change from the poetic manner of the eighteenth century, and the abandonment of the poetry of direct didacticism. The characteristic poetry of the nineteenth century was as different from that of the eighteenth century as the pictures of Turner were from those of the English pre-Raphaelites. That is to say, the typical poetry of the earlier age was marked by a clean symmetry, a clearness of imagery, and a sharpness of detail paralleled in some degree by the pictures of the pre-Raphaelites; whereas the poetry of the nineteenth century leaned more to imaginative embroidery, and what one may call, perhaps, the indefiniteness occasioned by artistic introspection. It was, in fact, very much in the nature of a change from a public oration to a private soliloquy. Even the mention, in nineteenth century poetry, of a great man's name to typify in a measure the greatness of his country, is unusual. In Wordsworth's sonnet, "It is not to be thought of," for example, the names of Shakespeare and Milton come as something of a surprise from the poet who did most to introduce the nineteenth century school of poetry. It is curious to note that here the poet unconsciously imitates the manner of the verse from which he deemed it his mission to effect a change; this sonnet is, indeed, curiously typical of the period of poetic reformation in which it was composed; for, though it belongs distinctly to the new school, it possesses in the references to Shakespeare and Milton one of the prominent characteristics of eighteenth century poetry. Thus, though the poetry of the third period contains poems of the highest order in direct praise of Shakespeare, as witness the sonnets of Mr. Swinburne and Matthew Arnold, it is apparent that the anthologist will find the greater part of his material in the works of prose writers. At first glance one is bewildered by the mass of literature which presents itself, but the scheme of this collection goes a small way towards simplifying the choice. Pieces dealing with particular merits of Shakespeare have generally been rejected, so that studies of characters in the plays find no place. Similarly, studies, such, for example, as De Quincey's fine psychological analysis of the knocking at the gate in *Macbeth*, have been excluded. Still, even with these limitations, one feels that the task of selection is beset with dangers. Every reader of Shakespearean literature has his favourite passages, and though I have endeavoured to judge with a just catholicity, I present the result of my labours in all meekness.

VI
SCHEME OF THE BOOK

The extracts have been arranged in three divisions. The first, which is subdivided into three periods, corresponding with those described in the foregoing notes, contains pieces in direct praise of Shakespeare.

The second part of the work contains brief passages in prose and verse similar in character to those in the first part, but selected either for their epigrammatic terseness or for their crystallisation of a fine thought that is conveniently detachable from its context.

The third part is devoted to pieces which treat Shakespeare or his works from a romantic standpoint. The devotion of only a small space to this section was inevitable, and I regret the number of omissions. One especially must be mentioned. Landor's witty *Citation and Examination of William Shakespeare* on the charge of deer stealing, represents exactly the kind of piece which I aimed at including. It is, however, far too long to quote in full, and the interest is so deftly carried throughout that I have found it quite impossible to select any portion which could stand intelligibly by itself. I should have liked, also, to include Browning's poem, *At the Mermaid*, but here the question of copyright intervened.

The dates immediately following the authors' names show (sometimes approximately) the earliest years with which the pieces quoted can be definitely associated. Occasionally they mark the year in which the piece was written, but in the majority of cases the year is that of publication.

My best thanks are due to the following authors and publishers, who have kindly given me permission to use copyright pieces:—Mr. A. C. Swinburne, Mr. W. M. Rossetti, Mr. Gerald Massey, Mr. Theodore Watts-Dunton, Mr. William Watson, Mr. Richard Watson Gilder, Mr. W. S. Gilbert, Dr. Ludwig Mond (Mathilde Blind), Messrs. Macmillan & Co. (Francis Turner Palgrave, Matthew Arnold, and John Henry Newman), Messrs. Ellis & Elvey (Dante Gabriel Rossetti), Messrs. George Allen & Son (John Ruskin), Messrs. Smith Elder & Co. (Robert Browning).

Finally, it is my pleasant duty to record my deep indebtedness to Mr. Sidney Lee, at whose suggestion this book was undertaken.

C. E. H.

PART I
"THESE THREE HUNDRED YEARS"

Any time these three hundred years.

Merry Wives, I. i. 13.

> When wasteful war shall statues overturn,
>
> And broils root out the work of masonry,
>
> Nor Mars his sword nor war's quick fire shall burn
>
> The living record of your memory.
>
> 'Gainst death and all-oblivious enmity
>
> Shall you pace forth; your praise shall still find room,
>
> Even in the eyes of all posterity
>
> That wear this world out to the ending doom.

Sonnet LV.

THE FIRST PERIOD
SIXTEENTH AND SEVENTEENTH
CENTURIES

FRANCIS MERES, 1596
(1565-1647)

AS the soul of Euphorbus was thought to live in Pythagoras, so the sweet witty soul of Ovid lives in mellifluous and honey-tongued Shakespeare, witness his "Venus and Adonis," his "Lucrece," his sugared sonnets among his private friends, etc.

As Plautus and Seneca are accounted the best for Comedy and Tragedy among the Latins, so Shakespeare among the English is the most excellent in both kinds for the stage; for Comedy, witness his "Gentlemen of Verona," his "Errors," his "Love's Labour's Lost," his "Love's Labour's Wonne," his "Midsummer Night's Dream," and his "Merchant of Venice"; for Tragedy, his "Richard the 2," "Richard the 3," "Henry the 4," "King John," "Titus Andronicus," and his "Romeo and Juliet."

As Epius Stolo said that the Muses would speak with Plautus' tongue, if they would speak Latin; so I say that the Muses would speak with Shakespeare's fine filed phrase, if they would speak English.

Palladis Tamia. Wits Treasury, Being the Second Part of Wits Commonwealth. 1598.

RICHARD BARNFIELD, 1598
(1574-1627)

"A Remembrance of some English Poets."

> AND Shakespeare thou, whose honey-flowing Vein
>
> (Pleasing the World), thy Praises doth obtain.
>
> Whose *Venus*, and whose *Lucrece* (sweet, and chaste)
>
> Thy Name in Fame's immortal Book have placed.
>
> Live ever you, at least in Fame live ever:
>
> Well may the Body die, but Fame dies never.

Poems in Divers humors. 1598. Sig. E2, back.

JOHN WEEVER, 1599
(1576-1632)

"Ad Gulielmum Shakespeare."

> HONEY-TONGUED Shakespeare, when I saw thine issue,
>
> I swore Apollo got them and none other;
>
> Their rosy-tinted features clothed in tissue,
>
> Some heaven-born goddess said to be their mother:
>
> Rose-cheeked *Adonis*, with his amber tresses,
>
> Fair fire-hot *Venus*, charming him to love her,
>
> Chaste *Lucretia*, virgin-like her dresses,
>
> Proud lust-stung *Tarquin*, seeking still to prove her:
>
> Romeo, Richard; more whose names I know not,
>
> Their sugared tongues, and power attractive beauty
>
> Say they are saints, although that saints they show not,
>
> For thousands vow to them subjective duty:
>
> They burn in love, thy children, Shakespeare het them,
> [heated
>
> Go, woo thy Muse, more Nymphish brood beget them.

Epigrammes in the oldest Cut, and newest Fashion. John Weever. 1599. Epig. 22.

Some bibliographers have assigned the first edition of Weever's *Epigrammes* to the year 1595, but no copy bearing that date is known.

JOHN DAVIES, 1610
(1565?-1618)

"To our English Terence, Mr. Will. Shakespeare."

> SOME say, good Will, which I in sport do sing,
>
> Had'st thou not play'd some kingly parts in sport,
>
> Thou had'st been a companion for a king,

And been a king among the meaner sort.

Some others rail; but rail as they think fit,

Thou hast no railing, but a reigning wit:

And honesty thou sow'st which they do reap;

So, to increase their stock which they do keep:

The Scourge of Folly, consisting of Satyricall Epigramms and others. 1611.

THOMAS FREEMAN, 1614
(*fl.* 1614)

"To Master W. Shakespeare."

> SHAKESPEARE, that nimble Mercury thy brain
>
> Lulls many hundred Argus-eyes asleep,
>
> So fit, for all thou fashionest thy rein,
>
> At th' horse-foot fountain thou hast drank full deep,
>
> Vertues or vices theme to thee all one is:
>
> Who loves chaste life, there's *Lucrece* for a Teacher:
>
> Who but read lust there's *Venus and Adonis*,
>
> True model of a most lascivious leacher.
>
> Besides in plays thy wit winds like Meander:
>
> Whence needy new-composers borrow more
>
> Than Terence doth from Plautus or Menander.
>
> But to praise thee aright I want thy store:
>
> Then let thine own works thine own worth upraise,
>
> And help t' adorn thee with deserved Bays.

Runne, and a Great Caste. The Second Bowle. (*Being the second part of a Rubbe, and a Great Cast*, 1614.) Epigram 92, Sig. K2, back.

WILLIAM BASSE, 1622
(*d.* 1653?)

RENOWNED Spenser lie a thought more nigh

To learned Beaumont, and rare Beaumont lie

A little nearer Chaucer, to make room

For Shakespeare in your threefold, fourfold tomb.

To lodge all four in one bed make a shift

Until Doom's day, for hardly will (a) fift

Betwixt this day and that by fate be slain,

For whom the curtains shall be drawn again.

For if precedency in death do bar

A fourth place in your sacred sepulchre,

In this uncarved marble of thy own,

Sleep, brave Tragedian, Shakespeare, sleep alone;

Thy unmolested rest, unshared cave,

Possess as lord, not tenant, to the grave,

That unto others it may counted be

Honour hereafter to be layed by thee.

Fennell's Shakespere Repository, 1853, p. 10. Printed from a MS. *temp.* Charles I.

ANONYMOUS, 1623

Judicio Pylium, genio Socratem, arte Maronem, Terra tegit, populus maeret, Olympus habet.

STAY, passenger, who goest thou by so fast?

Read, if thou canst, whom envious death hath placed

Within this monument; Shakespeare with whom

Quick nature died; whose name doth deck this tomb

Far more than cost; sith all that he hath writ

Leaves living art but page to serve his wit.

Inscription on the Monument erected to Shakespeare's Memory in the Parish Church at Stratford-on-Avon. 1623.

BEN JONSON, 1623
(1573-1637)

"To the memory of my beloved, the Author, Mr. William Shakespeare: and what he hath left us."

TO draw no envy, Shakespeare, on thy name,

Am I thus ample to thy book, and fame:

While I confess thy writings to be such,

As neither Man, nor Muse, can praise too much.

'Tis true, and all men's suffrage. But these ways

Were not the paths I meant unto thy praise:

For seeliest Ignorance on these may light,

Which, when it sounds at best, but echoes right;

Or blind Affection, which doth ne'er advance

The truth, but gropes, and urgeth all by chance;

Or crafty Malice, might pretend this praise,

And think to ruin, where it seem'd to raise . . .

But thou art proof against them, and in deed

Above th' ill fortune of them, or the need.

I, therefore, will begin. Soul of the age!

The applause! delight! the wonder of our stage!

My Shakespeare, rise; I will not lodge thee by

Chaucer, or Spenser, or bid Beaumont lie

A little further to make thee a room:

Thou art a monument, without a tomb,

And art alive still, while thy book doth live,

And we have wits to read, and praise to give.

That I not mix thee so, my brain excuses;

I mean with great, but disproportion'd Muses:

For, if I thought my judgment were of years,

I should commit thee surely with thy peers,

And tell how for thou didst our Lyly out-shine,

Or sporting Kid, or Marlowe's mighty line.

And though thou hadst small Latin, and less Greek,

From thence to honour thee, I would not seek

For names; but call forth thundering Æschilus,

Euripides, and Sophocles to us,

Paccuvius, Accius, him of Cordova dead,

To life again, to hear thy buskin tread,

And shake a stage: or, when thy socks were on,

Leave thee alone, for the comparison

Of all that insolent Greece or haughty Rome

Sent forth, or since did from their ashes come.

Triumph, my Britain, thou hast one to show,

To whom all scenes of Europe homage owe.

He was not of an age, but for all time!

And all the Muses still were in their prime,

When like Apollo he came forth to warm

Our ears, or like a Mercury to charm!

Nature herself was proud of his designs,

And joy'd to wear the dressing of his lines!

Which were so richly spun, and woven so fit,

As, since, she will vouchsafe no other wit.

The merry Greek, tart Aristophanes,

Neat Terence, witty Plautus, now not please;

But antiquated and deserted lie

As they were not of Nature's family.

Yet must I not give Nature all: thy Art,

My gentle Shakespeare, must enjoy a part.

For though the Poet's matter, Nature be,

His Art doth give the fashion. And, that he,

Who casts to write a living line, must sweat

(Such as thine are), and strike the second heat

Upon the Muse's anvil: turn the same

(And himself in it) that he thinks to frame;

Or for the laurel, he may gain a scorn,

For a good Poet's made, as well as born.

And such wert thou. Look how the father's face

Lives in his issue, even so, the race

Of Shakespeare's mind and manners brightly shines

In his well turned and true-filed lines:

In each of which he seems to shake a lance,

As brandish'd at the eyes of Ignorance.

Sweet Swan of Avon! what a sight it were

To see thee in our waters yet appear,

And make those flights upon the banks of Thames,

That so did take Eliza, and our James!

But stay, I see thee in the hemisphere

Advanced, and made a constellation there!

Shine forth, thou Star of Poets, and with rage,

Or influence, chide, or cheer the drooping Stage;

Which, since thy flight from hence, hath mourn'd like night,

And despairs day, but for thy volume's light.

Prefixed to the First Folio Edition of Shakespeare's *Works*.

... "I will not lodge thee by

Chaucer, or Spenser, or bid Beaumont lie

A little further to make thee a room."

See <u>William Basse</u>, p. 40.

HUGH HOLLAND, 1623
(*d.* 1633)

"Upon the Lines and Life of the famous Scenick Poet, Master William Shakespeare."

> THOSE hands, which you so clapt, go now, and wring
>
> You Britain's brave; for done are Shakespeare's days:
>
> His days are done, that made the dainty Plays,
>
> Which make the Globe of heav'n and earth to ring.
>
> Dried is that vein, dried is the Thespian Spring,
>
> Turn'd all to tears, and Phœbus clouds his rays:
>
> That corpse, that coffin now bestick those bayes,
>
> Which crown'd him Poet first, then Poet's King.
>
> If Tragedies might any Prologue have,
>
> All those he made, would scarce make one to this:
>
> Where Fame, now that he gone is to the grave
>
> (Death's public tiring-house), the Nuncius is.
>
> For though his line of life went soon about,
>
> The life yet of his lines shall never out.

Prefixed to the First Folio Edition of Shakespeare's *Works.*

JOHN HEMINGE, 1623
(*d.* 1630)

HENRIE CONDELL
(*d.* 1627)

"To the great Variety of Readers."

HIS mind and hand went together: and what he thought he uttered with that easiness, that we have scarce received from him a blot in his papers. But it is not our province, who only gather his works, and give them you, to praise him. It is yours that read him. And there we hope, to your divers capacities, you will find enough, both to draw, and hold you: for his wit can no more lie hid, than it could be lost. Read him, therefore; and again, and again: and if then you do not like him, surely you are in some manifest danger, not to understand him. And so we leave you to other of his friends, whom, if you need, can be your guides: if you need them not, you can lead yourselves, and others. And such readers we wish him.

Address prefixed to the First Folio Edition of Shakespeare's *Works.* 1623.

LEONARD DIGGES, 1623
(1588-1635)

"To the Memorie of the deceased Author, Maister W. Shakespeare."

> SHAKESPEARE, at length thy pious fellows give
>
> The world thy Works: thy Works, by which, out-live
>
> Thy Tomb, thy name must: when that stone is rent,
>
> And Time dissolves thy Stratford Monument,
>
> Here we alive shall view thee still. This Book,
>
> When brass and marble fade, shall make thee look
>
> Fresh to all ages: when posterity
>
> Shall loath what's new, thinke all is prodigy
>
> That is not Shakespeare's; ev'ry line, each verse,
>
> Here shall revive, redeem thee from thy hearse.
>
> Nor fire, nor cankering age, as Naso said,
>
> Of his, thy wit-fraught Book, shall once invade.
>
> Nor shall I e'er believe, or think thee dead
>
> (Though missed), until our bankrout Stage be sped
>
> (Impossible) with some new strain t' out-do
>
> Passions of Juliet, and her Romeo;

Or till I hear a scene more nobly take,

Then when thy half-sword parling Romans spake,

Till these, till any of thy Volumes rest

Shall with more fire, more feeling be expressed,

Be sure, our Shakespeare, thou canst never die,

But crown'd with laurel, live eternally.

Prefixed to the First Folio Edition of Shakespeare's *Works*. 1623.

MICHAEL DRAYTON, 1627
(1563-1631)

"To my most dearly-loved friend Henery Reynolds, Esquire, of Poets and Poesie."

SHAKESPEARE, thou hadst as smooth a comic vein,

Fitting the sock, and in thy natural brain,

As strong conception, and as clear a rage

As any one that trafick'd with the stage.

Elegies at the end of *The Battaile of Agincourt*. 1627, p. 206.

JOHN MILTON, 1630
(1608-1674)

"An Epitaph on the Admirable Dramatic Poet, W. Shakespeare."

WHAT needs my Shakespeare for his honour'd bones,

The labour of an age in pilèd stones?

Or that his hallow'd relics should be hid

Under a star-ypointing pyramid?

Dear son of Memory, great heir of Fame,

What need'st thou such weak witness of thy name?

Thou, in our wonder and astonishment,

Hast built thyself a life-long monument.

For whilst, to the shame of slow-endeavouring art,

Thy easy numbers flow; and that each heart

Hath, from the leaves of thy unvalued book,

Those Delphic lines with deep impression took;

Then thou, our fancy of itself bereaving,

Dost make us marble with too much conceiving;

And, so sepulchr'd, in such pomp dost lie,

That kings, for such a tomb should wish to die.

Prefixed to Second Folio Edition of Shakespeare's *Works*. 1632.

I. M. S., 1632

"On worthy Master Shakespeare and his Poems."

A MIND reflecting ages past, whose clear

And equal surface can make things appear

Distant a thousand years, and represent

Them in their lively colours' just extent.

To outrun hasty time, retrieve the fates,

Roll back the heavens, blow ope the iron gates

Of death and Lethe, where (confused) lie

Great heaps of ruinous mortality.

In that deep dusky dungeon to discern

A royal ghost from churls: by art to learn

The physiognomy of shades, and give

Them sudden birth, wond'ring how oft they live.

What story coldly tells, what poets feign

At second hand, and picture without brain

Senseless and soulless shows. To give a stage

(Ample and true with life) voice, action, age,

As Plato's year and new scene of the world

Them unto us, or us to them had hurl'd.

To raise our ancient sovereigns from their herse,

Make kings his subjects, by exchanging verse

Enlive their pale trunks, that the present age

Joys in their joy, and trembles at their rage:

Yet so to temper passion, that our ears

Take pleasure in their pain; and eyes in tears

Both weep and smile; fearful at plots so sad,

Then, laughing at our fear; abus'd, and glad

To be abus'd, affected with that truth

Which we perceive is false; pleas'd in that ruth

At which we start; and by elaborate play

Tortur'd and tickled; by a crablike way

Time past made pastime, and in ugly sort

Disgorging up his ravaine for our sport—

—While the Plebeian Imp, from lofty throne,

Creates and rules a world, and works upon

Mankind by secret engines; now to move

A chilling pity, then a rigorous love:

To strike up and stroke down, both joy and ire;

To steer th' affections; and by heavenly fire

Mould us anew. Stol'n from ourselves—

This, and much more which cannot be express'd,

But by himself, his tongue and his own breast,

Was Shakespeare's freehold, which his cunning brain

Improv'd by favour of the ninefold train.

The buskin'd Muse, the Comic Queen, the grand

And louder tone of Clio; nimble hand,

And nimbler foot of the melodious pair,

The silver voiced Lady; the most fair

Calliope, whose speaking silence daunts,

And she whose praise the heavenly body chants.

These jointly woo'd him, envying one another

(Obey'd by all as spouse, but lov'd as brother),

And wrought a curious robe of sable grave,

Fresh green, and pleasant yellow, red most brave,

And constant blue, rich purple, guiltless white,

The lowly russet, and the scarlet bright;

Branch'd and embroider'd like the painted Spring,

Each leaf match'd with a flower, and each string

Of golden wire, each line of silk; there run

Italian works whose thread the Sisters spun;

And there did sing, or seem to sing, the choice

Birds of a foreign note and various voice.

Here hangs a mossy rock; there plays a fair

But chiding fountain purled; not the air,

Nor clouds nor thunder, but were living drawn,

Not out of common tiffany or lawn,

But fine materials, which the Muses know,

And only know the countries where they grow.

Now, when they could no longer him enjoy

In mortal garments pent, death may destroy,

They say, his body, but his verse shall live;

And more than nature takes, our hands shall give.

In a less volume, but more strongly bound,

Shakespeare shall breath and speak, with laurel crown'd

Which never fades. Fed with Ambrosian meat,

In a well-lined vesture rich and neat.

So with this robe they clothe him, bid him wear it;

For time shall never stain, nor envy tear it.

The friendly admirer of his Endowments,
I. M. S.
Prefixed to the Second Folio Edition of
Shakespeare's *Works*. 1632.

Conjectures as to the authorship of this poem have been numerous.
Coleridge in his *Lectures on Shakespeare* says: "This poem is subscribed I. M.
S., meaning, as some have explained, the initials "John Milton, Student":
the internal evidence seems to us decisive; for there was, I think, no other
man, of that particular day, capable of writing anything so characteristic of
Shakespeare, so justly thought, and so happily expressed."

JOHN HALES, **BEFORE** 1633
(1584-1656)

IN a conversation between Sir John Suckling, Sir William D'Avenant,
Endymion Porter, Mr. Hales of Eton, and Ben Jonson, Sir John Suckling,
who was a professed admirer of Shakespeare, had undertaken his defence
against Ben Jonson with some warmth. Mr. Hales, who had sat still for
some time, hearing Ben frequently reproaching him with the want of
learning, and ignorance of the ancients, told him at last, "That if Mr.
Shakespeare had not read the ancients, he had likewise not stolen anything
from 'em [a fault the other made no conscience of]; and that if he would
produce any one topic finely treated by any of them, he would undertake to
show something upon the same subject at least as well written by
Shakespeare."

Some Account of the Life of Mr. William Shakespeare, prefixed to the
edition of his *Works* by Nicholas Rowe, 1709, vol. i. p. xiv.

SIR WILLIAM D'AVENANT, 1637
(1606-1668)

"Ode. In Remembrance of Master William Shakespeare."

1

> BEWARE (delighted Poets!) when you sing
>
> To welcome Nature in the early Spring;
>
> Your num'rous feet not tread

The Banks of Avon; for each flower

(As it ne'er knew a sun or shower)

Hangs there the pensive head.

      2

Each tree whose thick and spreading growth hath made

Rather a night beneath the boughs, than shade

(Unwilling now to grow),

Looks like the plume a captive wears

Whose rifled falls are steept i' th' tears

Which from his last rage flow.

      3

The piteous river wept itself away

Long since (alas!) to such a swift decay;

That reach the map; and look

If you a river there can spy;

And for a river your mock'd eye

Will find a shallow brook.

Madagascar, with other Poems. 1638, p. 37. Printed 1637.

ANONYMOUS, **ABOUT** 1637

"An Elegie on the Death of that famous Writer and Actor, Mr. William Shakspeare."

I DARE not do thy memory that wrong,

Unto our larger griefs to give a tongue;

I'll only sigh in earnest, and let fall

My solemn tears at thy great funeral;

For every eye that rains a show'r for thee,

Laments thy loss in a sad elegy.

Nor is it fit each humble Muse should have

Thy worth his subject, now th' art laid in grave;

No, it's a flight beyond the pitch of those,

Whose worthless pamphlets are not sense in prose.

Let learned Jonson sing a Dirge for thee,

And fill our Orb with mournful harmony:

But we need no remembrancer; thy fame

Shall still accompany thy honoured name

To all posterity; and make us be

Sensible of what we lost in losing thee:

Being the age's wonder, whose smooth rhymes

Did more reform than lash the looser times.

Nature herself did her own self admire,

As oft as thou wert pleased to attire

Her in her native lustre, and confess

Thy dressing was her chiefest comliness.

How can we then forget thee, when the age

Her chiefest tutor, and the widowed stage

Her only favourite in thee hath lost,

And Nature's self what she did brag of most?

Sleep then, rich soul of numbers, whilst poor we

Enjoy the profits of thy legacy;

And thinke it happiness enough we have

So much of thee redeemèd from the grave,

As may suffice to enlighten future times

With the bright lustre of thy matchless rhymes.

Appended to Shakespeare's *Poems*. 1640. Sig. L.

THOMAS BANCROFT, 1639
(*fl.* 1633-1658)

"To Shakespeare."

> THY Muse's sugared dainties seem to us
>
> Like the fam'd apples of old Tantalus:
>
> For we, admiring, see and hear thy strains;
>
> But none I see or hear, those sweets attains.

"To the same."

> Thou hast so us'd thy pen (or shook thy spear),
>
> That Poets startle, nor thy wit come near.

Two Bookes of Epigrammes, and Epitaphs. 1639. Nos. 118 and 119.

GEORGE DANIEL, 1647
(1616-1657)

> THE sweetest Swan of Avon, to ye fair
>
> And cruel Delia, passionately sings;
>
> Other men's weaknesses and follies are
>
> Honour and wit to him; each accent brings
>
> A sprig to crown him Poet; and contrive
>
> A monument, in his own work, to live.

Poems. Vindication of Poesie. Add. MS. 19255, p. 17. (British Museum.) Privately printed by Dr. Grosart. 1878, 4 vols. Vol. i. pp. 28, 29.

SAMUEL SHEPPARD, 1651
(*fl. c.* 1606-1652)

"In Memory of our Famous Shakespeare."

1

> SACRED spirit, whiles thy Lyre

Echoed o'er the Arcadian Plains,
Even Apollo did admire,
Orpheus wondered at thy strains.

2

Plautus sigh'd, Sophocles wept
Tears of anger, for to hear,
After they so long had slept,
So bright a genius should appear.

3

Who wrote his Lines with a sun-beam,
More durable than Time or Fate;
Others boldly do blaspheme,
Like those that seem to preach, but prate.

4

Thou wert truly priest elect,
Chosen darling to the Nine;
Such a trophy to erect
By thy wit and skill divine.

5

That were all their other glories
(Thine excepted) torn away,
By thy admirable stories,
Their garments ever shall be gay.

6

Where thy honoured bones do lie

(As Statius once to Maro's urn),

Thither every year will I

Slowly tread, and sadly mourn.

Epigrams Theological, Philosophical, and Romantick. Six Books, etc., with other Select Poems. 1651. Book vi. Epig. 17, pp. 150, 152, 154.

THOMAS FULLER, *c.* 1661
(1608-1661)

HE was an eminent instance of the truth of that rule, *Poeta non fit sed nascitur,* one is not *made,* but *born* a poet. Indeed, his learning was very little, so that, as Cornish diamonds are not polished by any lapidary, but are pointed and smoothed even as they are taken out of the earth, so nature itself was all the *art* which was used upon him.

Many were the wit-combats betwixt him and Ben Jonson; which two I behold like a Spanish great galleon and an English man of war: Master Jonson (like the former) was built far higher in learning; solid, but slow in his performances. Shakespeare, with the English man of war, lesser in bulk, but lighter in sailing, could turn with all tides, tack about, and take advantage of all winds, by the quickness of his wit and invention.

The History of the Worthies of England: Warwickshire. 1662, p. 126.

SAMUEL PEPYS, 1662-1667
(1633-1703)

1661-1662. March 1st. My wife and I by coach, first to see my little picture that is a-drawing, and thence to the Opera, and there saw "Romeo and Juliet," the first time it was ever acted, but it is a play of itself the worst that ever I heard, and the worst acts that ever I saw these people do, and I am resolved to go no more to see the first time of acting, for they were all of them out more or less.

1662. September 29th. To the King's Theatre, where we saw "Midsummer Night's Dream," which I had never seen before, nor ever shall again, for it is the most insipid, ridiculous play that ever I saw in my life.

1666. December 28th. To the Duke's House, and there saw "Macbeth" most excellently acted, and a most excellent play for variety. I had sent my wife to meet me there, who did come: so I did go to White Hall, and got my Lord Bellassis to get me into the playhouse; and there, after all staying above an hour for the players, the King and all waiting, which was absurd, saw "Henry the Fifth" well done by the Duke's people, and in most excellent habit, all new vests, being put on but this night. But I sat so high and far off, that I missed most of the words, and sat with a wind coming into my back and neck, which did much trouble me. The play continued till twelve at night; and then up, and a most horrid cold night it was, and frosty, and moonshine.

1666-67. January 7th. To the Duke's House, and saw "Macbeth," which, though I saw it lately, yet appears a most excellent play in all respects, but especially in divertisement, though it be a deep tragedy; which is a strange perfection in a tragedy, it being most proper here, and suitable.

1667. October 16th. To the Duke of York's House; and I was vexed to see Young, who is but a bad actor at best, act Macbeth, in the room of Betterton, who, poor man! is sick: but, Lord! what a prejudice it wrought in me against the whole play, and everybody else agreed in disliking this fellow. Thence home, and there find my wife gone home; because of this fellow's acting of the part, she went out of the house again.

Diary and Correspondence of Samuel Pepys, with a Life and Notes, by Richard, Lord Braybrooke. 1888.

MARGARET CAVENDISH, DUCHESS OF NEWCASTLE, 1664 (1624?-1674)

I WONDER how that person you mention in your letter could either have the conscience, or confidence to dispraise Shakespeare's plays, as to say they were made up only with clowns, fools, watchmen, and the like; but to answer that person, though Shakespeare's wit will answer for himself, I say, that it seems by his judging, or censuring, he understands not plays, or wit; for to express properly, rightly, usually, and naturally, a clown's, or fool's humour, expressions, phrases, garbs, manners, actions, words, and course of life, is as witty, wise, judicious, ingenious, and observing, as to write and express the expressions, phrases, garbs, manners, actions, words, and course of life, of kings and princes; and to express naturally, to the life, a mean country wench, as a great lady; a courtesan, as a chaste woman; a mad man, as a man in his right reason and senses; a drunkard, as a sober man; a knave, as an honest man; and so a clown, as a well-bred man; and a fool, as a wise man; nay, it expresses and declares a greater wit, to express, and deliver to posterity, the extravagances of madness, the subtlety of knaves, the ignorance of clowns, and the simplicity of naturals, or the craft of feigned fools, than to express regularities, plain honesty, courtly garbs, or sensible discourses, for 'tis harder to express nonsense than sense, and ordinary conversations, than that which is unusual; and 'tis harder, and requires more wit to express a jester, than a grave statesman; yet Shakespeare did not want wit to express to the life all sorts of persons, of what quality, profession, degree, breeding, or birth soever; nor did he want wit to express the divers and different humours, or natures or several passions in mankind; and so well he hath expressed in his plays all sorts of persons, as one would think he had been transformed into every one of those persons he hath described. . . . Who could not swear he had been a noble lover, that could woo so well? and there is not any person he had described in his book, but his readers might think they were well acquainted with them; indeed, Shakespeare had a clear judgment, a quick wit, a spreading fancy, a subtle observation, a deep apprehension, and a most eloquent elocution; truly he was a natural orator, as well as a natural poet, and he was not an orator to speak well only on some subjects, as lawyers, who can make eloquent orations at the bar, and plead subtly and wittily in law-cases, or divines, that can preach eloquent sermons, or dispute subtly and wittily in theology, but take them from that, and put them to other subjects, and they will be to seek; but Shakespeare's wit and eloquence was general, for and upon all subjects, he rather wanted subjects for his wit and eloquence to work on, for which he was forced to take some of his plots out of history, where he only took the bare designs, the wit and language being all his own.

CCXI Sociable Letters written by the Lady Marchioness of Newcastle. 1664. Letter CXXIII.

JOHN DRYDEN, 1667
(1631-1700)

> AS when a tree's cut down, the secret root
>
> Lives under ground, and thence new branches shoot;
>
> So, from old Shakespeare's honour'd dust, this day
>
> Springs up and buds a new reviving play.
>
> Shakespeare who, taught by none, did first impart
>
> To Fletcher wit, to labouring Jonson art.
>
> He, monarch-like, gave those his subjects law,
>
> And is that Nature which they paint and draw.
>
> Fletcher reach'd that which on his heights did grow,

Whilst Jonson crept and gather'd all below.

This did his love, and this his mirth digest:

One imitates him most, the other best.

If they have since out-writ all other men,

'Tis with the drops which fell from Shakespeare's pen.

The storm which vanish'd on the neighb'ring shore,

Was taught by Shakespeare's *Tempest* first to roar.

That innocence and beauty which did smile

In Fletcher, grew on this Enchanted Isle.

But Shakespeare's magick could not copy'd be,

Within that circle none durst walk but he.

I must confess 'twas bold, nor would you now

That liberty to vulgar wits allow,

Which works by magick supernatural things:

But Shakespeare's pow'r is sacred as a king's.

Those legends from old priesthood were receiv'd,

And he then writ, as people then believed.

Prologue to the Tempest or the Enchanted Island, by Sir William D'Avenant and John Dryden. 1676.

See also Dryden's *Prologue to Troilus and Cressida*, spoken by Mr. Betterton representing the Ghost of Shakespeare.

1668

TO begin, then, with Shakespeare; he was the man who of all modern, and perhaps ancient poets, had the largest and most comprehensive soul. All the images of nature were still present to him, and he drew them not laboriously, but luckily: when he describes any thing, you more than see it, you feel it too. Those who accuse him to have wanted learning, give him the greater commendation: he was naturally learned; he needed not the spectacles of books to read Nature; he looked inwards, and found her there. I cannot say he is everywhere alike; were he so, I should do him injury to compare him with the greatest of mankind. He is many times flat, insipid; his comic wit degenerating into clenches, his serious swelling into bombast. But he is always great, when some great occasion is presented to him; no man can say he ever had a fit subject for his wit, and did not then raise himself as high above the rest of poets,

> Quantum lenta solent inter viberna cupressi.

Of Dramatic Poesie, an Essay, 1668, p. 47.

The following is from Dryden's *Defence of the Epilogue*:—Let any man who understands English read diligently the works of Shakespeare and Fletcher, and I dare undertake that he will find in every page either some solecism of speech, or some notorious flaw in sense; and yet these men are reverenced, when we are not forgiven. That their wit is great, and many times their expressions noble, envy itself cannot deny.

> ——Neque ego illis detrahere ausim
>
> Hærentem capiti multa cum laude coronam.

But the times were ignorant in which they lived. Poetry was then, if not in its infancy among us, at least not arrived to its vigour and maturity. Witness the lameness of their plots; many of which, especially those which they writ first (for even that age refined itself in some measure), were made up of some ridiculous incoherent story, which in one play many times took up the business of an age. I suppose I need not name "Pericles, Prince of Tyre," nor the historical plays of Shakespeare; besides many of the rest, as the "Winter's Tale," "Love's Labour's Lost," "Measure for Measure," which were either grounded on impossibilities, or at least so meanly written that the comedy neither caused your mirth, nor the serious part your concernment.

ANONYMOUS, 1672

> IN country beauties, as we often see
>
> Something that takes in their simplicity;
>
> Yet while they charm, they know not they are fair,
>
> And take without their spreading of the snare;
>
> Such artless beauty lies in Shakespeare's wit,
>
> 'Twas well in spite of him what ere he writ.

His excellencies came and were not sought,

His words like casual atoms made a thought:

Drew up themselves in rank and file, and writ,

He wond'ring how the Devil it were such wit.

Thus like the drunken tinker, in his play,

He grew a prince, and never knew which way.

He did not know what trope or figure meant,

But to persuade is to be eloquent;

So in this Cæsar which this day you see,

Tully ne'er spoke as he makes Anthony.

Those then that tax his learning are to blame,

He knew the thing, but did not know the name:

Great Jonson did that ignorance adore,

And though he envied much, admir'd him more.

The faultless Jonson equally writ well:

Shakespeare made faults; but then did more excell.

One close at guard like some old fencer lay,

T'other more open, but he show'd more play.

In imitation Jonson's wit was shown,

Heaven made his men but Shakespeare made his own.

Wise Jonson's talent in observing lay,

But other's follies still made up his play.

He drew the like in each elaborate line,

But Shakespeare, like a master, did design.

Jonson with skill dissected human kind,

And show'd their faults that they their faults might find.

But then, as all anatomists must do,

He to the meanest of mankind did go,

And took from gibbets such as he would show.

Both are so great that he must boldly dare,

Who both of 'em does judge and both compare.

If amongst poets, one more bold there be,

The man that dare attempt in either way, is he.

Covent Garden Drollery, or a Collection of all the Choice Songs, Poems, Prologues, and Epilogues (Sung and Spoken at Courts and Theaters), never in Print before. Written by the refined'st Witts of the Age, and collected by A. B. [? Alex. Brome]. 1672.

EDWARD PHILLIPS, 1675
(1630-1696?)

WILLIAM SHAKESPEARE, the glory of the English Stage; whose nativity at Stratford-upon-Avon is the highest honour that town can boast of: from an actor of tragedies and comedies, he became a maker; and such a maker, that though some others may perhaps pretend to a more exact decorum and economy, especially in tragedy, never any expressed a more lofty and tragic height, never any represented nature more purely to the life; and where the polishments of art are most wanting, as probably his learning was not extraordinary, he pleaseth with a certain wild and native elegance; and in all his writings hath an unvulgar style, as well in his *Venus and Adonis*, his *Rape of Lucrece*, and other various poems, as in his dramatics.

Theatrum Poetarum. 1675. Preface. *The Modern Poets*, p. 194.

THOMAS OTWAY, 1680
(1652-1685)

In ages past (when will those times renew?),

When empires flourish'd, so did poets too.

When great Augustus the world's empire held,

Horace and Ovid's happy verse excell'd.

Ovid's soft genius, and his tender arts

Of moving Nature, melted hardest hearts.

It did th' imperial beauty, Julia, move

To listen to the language of his love.

Her father honour'd him: and on her breast

With ravish'd sense in her embraces prest,

He lay transported, fancy-full and blest.

Horace's lofty genius boldlier rear'd

His manly head, and through all Nature steer'd;

Her richest pleasures in his verse refin'd,

And wrought 'em to the relish of the mind.

He lash'd with a true poet's fearless rage,

The villanies and follies of the age;

Therefore Mecænas, that great fav'rite rais'd

Him high, and by him was he highly prais'd.

Our Shakespeare wrote, too, in an age as blest,

The happiest poet of his time, and best;

A gracious Prince's favour cheer'd his muse,

A constant favour he ne'er fear'd to lose.

Therefore he wrote with fancy unconfin'd,

And thoughts that were immortal as his mind;

And from the crop of his luxuriant pen

E'er since succeeding poets humbly glean.

Prologue to the History and Fall of Caius Marius. A Tragedy. 1712.

"A PERSON OF HONOUR," 1681

I CAN'T, without infinite ingratitude to the memory of those excellent persons, omit the first famous masters in't, of our nation, venerable Shakespeare and the great Ben Jonson. I have had a particular kindness always for most of Shakespeare's tragedies, and for many of his comedies, and I can't but say that I can never enough admire his style (considering the time he writ in, and the great alteration that has been in the refining of our language since), for he has expressed himself so very well in't that 'tis generally approved of still; and for maintaining of the characters of the persons design'd, I think none ever exceeded him.

"An Essay on Dramatic Poetry" appended to *Amaryllis to Tityrus, Being the First Heroick Harangue of the excellent pen of Monsieur Scudery. A Witty and Pleasant Novel.* Englished by a Person of Honour, 1681, pp. 66-67.

SIR CHARLES SEDLEY, 1693
(1639?-1701)

> BUT against old as well as new to rage,
>
> Is the peculiar frenzy of this age.
>
> Shakespeare must down, and you must praise no more
>
> Soft Desdemona, nor the jealous Moor:
>
> Shakespeare whose fruitful genius, happy wit
>
> Was fram'd and finish'd at a lucky hit;
>
> The pride of Nature, and the shame of schools,
>
> Born to create, and not to learn from rules;
>
> Must please no more, his bastards now deride,
>
> Their father's nakedness they ought to hide,
>
> But when on spurs their Pegasus they force,
>
> Their jaded Muse is distanc'd in the course.

The Wary Widdow, or Sir Noisy Parrat. A Comedy. By Henry Higden. Prologue by Sir Charles Sydley. 1693.

THE SECOND PERIOD
THE EIGHTEENTH CENTURY

SIR RICHARD STEELE, 1709
(1672-1729)

THE play of "The London Cuckolds" was acted this evening before a suitable audience, who were extremely well diverted with that heap of vice and absurdity. The indignation which Eugenio, who is a gentleman of just taste, has, upon occasion of seeing human nature fall so low in their delights, made him, I thought, expatiate upon the mention of this play very agreeably. "Of all men living," said he, "I pity players (who must be men of good understanding to be capable of being such) that they are obliged to repeat and assume proper gestures for representing things, of which their reason must be ashamed, and which they must disdain their audience for approving. The amendment of these low gratifications is only to be made by people of condition, by encouraging the presentation of the noble characters drawn by Shakespeare and others, from whence it is impossible to return without strong impressions of honour and humanity. On these occasions distress is laid before us with all its causes and consequences, and our resentment placed according to the merit of the persons afflicted. Were dramas of this nature more acceptable to the taste of the town, men who have genius would bend their studies to excel in them."

The Tatler, No. 8, 28 April 1709.

The London Cuckolds, by Edward Ravenscroft, first produced 1682.

NICHOLAS ROWE, 1709
(1674-1718)

THE delicacy of his taste, and the natural bent of his own genius (equal, if not superior, to some of the best of theirs [the ancients]), would certainly have led him to read and study them with so much pleasure, that some of their fine images would naturally have insinuated themselves into, and been mixed with his own writings; so that his not copying at least something from them, may be an argument of his never having read them. Whether his ignorance of the ancients were a disadvantage to him or no, may admit of a dispute: for though the knowledge of them might have made him more correct, yet it is not improbable but that the regularity and deference for them, which would have attended that correctness, might have restrained some of that fire, impetuosity, and even beautiful extravagance, which we admire in Shakespeare: and I believe we were better pleased with those thoughts, altogether new and uncommon, which his own imagination supplied him so abundantly with, than if he had given us the most beautiful passages out of the Greek and Latin poets, and that in the most agreeable manner that it was possible for a master of the English language to deliver them.

Some Account of the Life, etc., of Mr. William Shakespear, p. iii. prefixed to *Works of Shakespeare*, ed. N. Rowe. 1709.

Of this passage and the question of Shakespeare's knowledge of the ancients, Theobald, who favoured the view that his acquaintance with classical writings was not inconsiderable, remarks in his preface, "The result of the controversy must certainly, either way, terminate to our author's honour: how happily he could imitate them, if that point be allowed; or how gloriously he could think like them, without owing anything to imitation."

ELIJAH FENTON, 1711
(1683-1730)

> SHAKESPEARE, the genius of our isle, whose mind
>
> (The universal mirror of mankind)
>
> Express'd all images, enrich'd the stage,
>
> But sometimes stoop'd to please a barbarous age.
>
> When his immortal bays began to grow,
>
> Rude was the language, and the humour low:
>
> He, like the God of Day, was always bright,
>
> But rolling in its course, his orb of light
>
> Was sullied, and obscur'd, though soaring high,
>
> With spots contracted from the nether sky.
>
> But whither is th' adventurous Muse betray'd?
>
> Forgive her rashness, venerable shade!
>
> May Spring with purple flowers perfume thy urn;
>
> And Avon with his greens thy grave adorn:

Be all thy faults, whatever faults there be,

Imputed to the times, and not to thee.

Some scions shot from this immortal root,

Their tops much lower, and less fair the fruit,

Jonson the tribute of my verse might claim,

Had he not strove to blemish Shakespeare's name.

But, like the radiant twins that gild the sphere,

Fletcher and Beaumont next in pomp appear:

The first a fruitful vine, in blooming pride,

Had been by superfluity destroy'd,

But that his friend, judiciously severe,

Prun'd the luxuriant boughs with artful care;

On various sounding harps the Muses play'd,

And sung, and quaff'd their nectar in the shade.

Few moderns in the lists with these may stand,

For in those days were giants in the land:

Suffice it now by lineal right to claim,

And bow with filial awe to Shakespeare's fame;

The second honours are a glorious name.

Achilles dead, they found no equal lord

To wear his armour, and to wield his sword.

An Epistle to Mr. Southerne, from Kent. January 28, 1710-11.

JOHN DENNIS, 1712
(1657-1734)

SHAKESPEARE was one of the greatest geniuses that the world e'er saw for the Tragic Stage. Though he lay under greater disadvantages than any of his successors, yet had he greater and more genuine beauties than the best and greatest of them. And what makes the brightest glory of his character, those beauties were entirely his own, and owing to the force of his own nature; whereas his faults were owing to his education, and to the age that he lived in. One may say of him as they did of Homer, that he had none to imitate, and is himself inimitable.

An Essay on the Genius and Writings of Shakespear: with some Letters of Criticism to the SPECTATOR. 1712, pp. 1, 2.

EDWARD YOUNG, 1712
(1683-1765)

> TO claim attention, and the heart invade,
>
> Shakespeare but *wrote* the play th' Almighty *made.*
>
> Our neighbour's stage art too bare-fac'd betrays,
>
> 'Tis great Corneille at every scene we praise;
>
> On nature's surer aid Britannia calls,
>
> None think of Shakespeare till the curtain falls;
>
> Then with a sigh returns our audience home,
>
> From Venice, Egypt, Persia, Greece, or Rome.
>
> .   .   .   .   .   .
>
> And yet in Shakespeare something still I find,
>
> That makes me less esteem all humankind;
>
> He made one nature and another found,
>
> Both in his page with master-strokes abound;
>
> His witches, fairies, and enchanted isle,
>
> Bid us no longer at our nurses smile;
>
> Of lost historians we almost complain,
>
> Nor think it the creation of his brain.

Epistle to the Right Honourable George, Lord Lansdowne. 1712, ll. 295-302 and 313-20.

JOSEPH ADDISON, 1714
(1672-1719)

OUR critics do not seem sensible that there is more beauty in the works of a great genius who is ignorant of the rules of art, than in those of a little genius who knows and observes them. It is of these men of genius that Terence speaks in opposition to the little artificial cavillers of his time:

> Quorum æmulari exoptat negligentiam
>
> Potius quam istorum obscuram diligentiam.

A critic may have the same consolation in the ill success of his play, as Dr. South tells us a physician has at the death of a patient, that he was killed *secundum artem*. Our inimitable Shakespeare is a stumbling-block to the whole tribe of these rigid critics. Who would not rather read one of his plays, where there is not a single rule of the stage observed, than any production of a modern critic, where there is not one of them violated? Shakespeare was indeed born with all the seeds of poetry, and may be compared to the stone in Pyrrhus's ring, which, as Pliny tells us, had the figure of Apollo and the nine Muses in the veins of it, produced by the spontaneous hand of Nature, without any help from art.

The Spectator, No. 592, 10 Feb. 1714.

ALEXANDER POPE, 1725
(1688-1744)

IF ever any author deserved the name of an *Original*, it was Shakespeare. Homer himself drew not his art so immediately from the fountains of Nature; it proceeded through Egyptian strainers and channels, and came to him not without some tincture of the learning, or some cast of the models, of those before him. The poetry of Shakespeare was inspiration indeed; he is not so much an imitator as an instrument of Nature: and it is not so just to say that he speaks from her, as that she speaks through him.

His *characters* are so much Nature herself, that 'tis a sort of injury to call them by so distant a name as copies of her. Those of other poets have a constant resemblance, which shows that they received them from one another, and were but multipliers of the same image; each picture, like a mock rainbow, is but the reflection of a reflection. But every single character in Shakespeare is as much an individual as those in life itself; it is as impossible to find any two alike; as such as from their relation or affinity in any respect appear most to be twins, will upon comparison be found remarkably distinct. To this life and variety of character we must add the wonderful preservation of it, which is such throughout his Plays, that, had all the speeches been printed without the very names of the persons, I believe one might have applied them with certainty to every speaker.

The power over our passions was never possessed in a more eminent degree, or displayed in so different instances. Yet all along there is seen no labour, no pains to raise them; no preparation to guide our guess to the effect, or be perceiv'd to lead toward it; but the heart swells, and the tears burst out, just at the proper places. We are surprised the moment we weep; and yet upon reflection find the passion so just, that we should be surprised if we had not wept, and wept at that very moment.

How astonishing is it, again, that the passions directly opposite to these, laughter and spleen, are no less at his command! that he is not more a master of the *great* than of the *ridiculous* in human nature; of our noblest tendernesses, than of our vainest foibles; of our strongest emotions, than of our idlest sensations!

Nor does he only excel in the passions: in the coolness of reflection and reasoning he is full as admirable. His *sentiments* are not only in general the most pertinent and judicious upon every subject; but by a talent very peculiar, something between penetration and felicity, he hits upon that particular point on which the bent of each argument turns, or the force of each motive depends. This is perfectly amazing, from a man of no education or experience in those great and public scenes of life which are usually the subject of his thoughts: so that he seems to have known the world by intuition, to have looked through human nature at one glance, and to be the only author that gives ground for a very new opinion: That the philosopher, and even the man of the world, may be *born*, as well as the poet.

It must be owned that with all these great excellencies, he has almost as great defects; and that as he has certainly written better, so he has perhaps written worse, than any other. But I think I can in some measure account for these defects, from several causes and accidents; without which it is hard to imagine that so large and so enlightened a mind could ever have been susceptible of them. That all these contingencies should unite to his disadvantage seems to me almost as singularly unlucky, as that so many various (nay contrary) talents should meet in one man, was happy and extraordinary.

....

I will conclude by saying of Shakespeare, that with all his faults, and with all the irregularity of his *drama*, one may look upon his works in comparison of those that are more finished and regular, as upon an ancient majestic piece of Gothic architecture compared with a neat modern building; the latter is more elegant and glaring, but the former is more strong and more solemn. It must be allowed, that in one of these there are materials enough to make many of the other. It has much the greater variety, and much the nobler apartments; though we are often conducted to them by dark, odd, and uncouth passages. Nor does the whole fail to strike us with greater reverence, though many of the parts are childish, ill-placed, and unequal to its grandeur.

Preface to *The Works of Shakespeare*. 1725.

De Quincey in his essay on Pope says of this preface: "For the edition we have little to plead; but for the editor it is but just to make three apologies. In the *first* place he wrote a brilliant preface, which, although (like other works of the same class) too much occupied in displaying his own ability, and too often, for the sake of an effective antithesis, doing deep injustice to Shakespeare, yet undoubtedly, as a whole, extended his fame, by giving the sanction and countersign of a great wit to the national admiration. *Secondly*, as Dr. Johnson admits, Pope's failure pointed out the right road to his successors. *Thirdly*, even in this failure it is but fair to say, that in a graduated scale of merit, as distributed amongst the long succession of editors through that century, Pope holds a rank proportionable to his age. For the year 1720, he is no otherwise below Theobald, Hanmer, Capell, Warburton, or even Johnson, than as they are successively below each other, and all of them as to accuracy below Steevens, as he again was below Malone and Reed."

JAMES THOMSON, 1727
(1700-1748)

> HAPPY Britannia! where the Queen of Arts,
>
> Inspiring vigour, Liberty abroad
>
> Walks unconfined, even to thy farthest cots,
>
> And scatters plenty with unsparing hand
>
> .   .   .   .   .   .
>
> Thy sons of glory many! Alfred thine,
>
> In whom the splendour of heroic war,
>
> And more heroic peace, when govern'd well,
>
> Combine; whose hallow'd name *the Virtues Saint*,
>
> And his own Muses love; the best of kings!
>
> .   .   .   .   .   .

Fair thy renown

In awful sages and in noble bards;

Soon as the light of dawning Science spread

Her orient ray, and waked the Muses' song.

. . . . . .

For lofty sense,

Creative fancy, and inspection keen

Through the deep windings of the human heart,

Is not wild Shakespeare thine and Nature's boast?

The Seasons: Summer. 1727, ll. 1442-6, 1479-83, 1531-4, and 1563-6.

LEWIS THEOBALD, 1733
(1688-1744)

IN how many points of light must we be obliged to gaze at this great poet! In how many branches of excellence to consider and admire him! Whether we view him on the side of art or nature, he ought equally to engage our attention; whether we respect the force and greatness of his genius, the extent of his knowledge and reading, the power and address with which he throws out and applies either nature or learning, there is ample scope both for our wonder and pleasure. If his diction and the clothing of his thoughts attract us, how much more must we be charmed with the richness and variety of his images and ideas! If his images and ideas steal into our souls, and strike upon our fancy, how much are they improved in price when we come to reflect with what propriety and justness they are applied to character. If we look into his characters, and how they are furnished and proportioned to the employment he cuts out for them, how are we taken up with the mastery of his portraits! What draughts of Nature! What variety of originals, and how differing each from the other! How are they dressed from the stores of his own luxurious imagination; without being the apes of mode, or borrowing from any foreign wardrobe! each of them are the standard of fashion for themselves: like gentlemen that are above the direction of their tailors, and can adorn themselves without the aid of imitation.

Preface to *The Works of Shakespeare, collated with the Oldest Copies and corrected; with Notes, Explanatory and Critical.* By Mr. Theobald. 1733, vol. i. pp. ii-iii.

JOSEPH WARTON, 1740
(1722-1800)

> WHAT are the lays of artful Addison,
>
> Coldly correct, to Shakespeare's warblings wild?
>
> Whom on the winding Avon's willow'd banks
>
> Fair Fancy found, and bore the smiling babe
>
> To a close cavern (still the shepherds show
>
> The sacred place, whence with religious awe
>
> They hear, returning from the field at eve,
>
> Strange whisp'rings of sweet music through the air):
>
> Here, as with honey gather'd from the rock
>
> She fed the little prattler, and with songs
>
> Oft sooth'd his wond'ring ears with deep delight.
>
> On her soft lap he sat, and caught the sounds.

The Enthusiast: or the Lover of Nature, ll. 168-79.

WILLIAM COLLINS, 1743
(1721-1759)

> TOO nicely Jonson knew the critic's part;
>
> Nature in him was almost lost in art.
>
> Of softer mould the gentle Fletcher came,
>
> The next in order, as the next in name:
>
> With pleas'd attention 'midst his scenes we find
>
> Each glowing thought that warms the female mind;
>
> Each melting sigh and every tender tear,
>
> The lover's wishes, and the virgin's fear.
>
> His every strain the smiles and graces own,
>
> But stronger Shakespeare felt for man alone:
>
> Drawn by his pen, our ruder passions stand

Th' unrival'd picture of his early hand.

Verses humbly address'd to Sir Thomas Hanmer on his Edition of Shakespeare's Works. 1743, p. 7.

Hanmer's edition of Shakespeare appeared in 1744. See p. 93.

SIR THOMAS HANMER, 1744
(1677-1746)

IF that rich vein of sense which runs through the works of this author can be retrieved in every part and brought to appear in its true light, and if it may be hoped without presumption that this is here effected; they who love and admire him will receive a new pleasure, and all probably will be more ready to join in doing him justice, who does great honour to his country as a rare and perhaps singular genius: one who hath attained an high degree of perfection in those two great branches of poetry, tragedy and comedy, different as they are in their natures from each other; and who may be said without partiality to have equalled, if not excelled, in both kinds, the best writers of any age or century who have thought it glory enough to distinguish themselves in either.

Preface to *The Works of Shakespear. Carefully Revised and Corrected by the former Editions, and Adorned with Sculptures designed and executed by the best hands.* Oxford, 1744, vol. i. pp. v-vi.

SAMUEL JOHNSON, 1747
(1709-1784)

> WHEN Learning's triumph o'er her barb'rous foes
>
> First rear'd the stage, immortal Shakespeare rose;
>
> Each change of many-coloured life he drew,
>
> Exhausted worlds, and then imagined new:
>
> Existence saw him spurn her bounded reign,
>
> And panting Time toil'd after him in vain:
>
> His powerful strokes presiding truth impress'd,
>
> And unresisted passion storm'd the breast.

Prologue spoken by Mr. Garrick at the opening of the Theatre in Drury Lane, 1747.

"Drinking tea one day at Garrick's with Mr. Langton, he [Dr. Johnson] was questioned if he was not somewhat of a heretic as to Shakespeare; said Garrick, 'I doubt he is a little of an infidel.'—'Sir,' said Johnson, 'I will stand by the lines I have written on Shakespeare in my Prologue at the opening of your Theatre.' Mr. Langton suggested, that in the line

"'And panting Time toil'd after him in vain,'

Johnson might have had in his eye the passage in the *Tempest*, where Prospero says of Miranda:

"'. . . She will outstrip all praise,

And make it halt behind her.'

Johnson said nothing. Garrick then ventured to observe, 'I do not think that the happiest line in the praise of Shakespeare.' Johnson exclaimed (smiling), 'Prosaical rogues! next time I write, I'll make both time and space pant.'"—Notes by Langton in Boswell's *Life of Dr. Johnson*.

BISHOP WILLIAM WARBURTON, 1747.
(1698-1779)

OF all the literary exercitations of speculative men, whether designed for the use or entertainment of the world, there are none of so much importance, or what are more our immediate concern, than those which let us into the knowledge of our nature. Others may exercise the reason or amuse the imagination; but these only can improve the heart, and form the human mind to wisdom. Now, in this science, our Shakespeare is confessed to occupy the foremost place; whether we consider the amazing sagacity with which he investigates every hidden spring and wheel of human action; or his happy manner of communicating this knowledge, in the just and living paintings which he has given us of all our passions, appetites, and pursuits. These afford a lesson which can never be too often repeated, or too constantly inculcated.

Preface to *The Works of Shakespear. The genuine Text (collated with all the former Editions and then corrected and emended) is here settled. Being restored from the Blunders of the first Editors, and the Interpolations of the two last. With a Comment and Notes, Critical and Explanatory.* By Mr. Pope and Mr. Warburton. 1747, vol. i. p. xxiv.

CHRISTOPHER SMART, 1751
(1722-1771)

> METHINKS I see with fancy's magic eye,
>
> The shade of Shakespeare, in yon azure sky.
>
> On yon high cloud behold the bard advance,
>
> Piercing all nature with a single glance:
>
> In various attitudes around him stand
>
> The passions, waiting for his dread command.
>
> First kneeling Love before his feet appears,
>
> And, musically sighing, melts in tears.
>
> Near him fell Jealousy with fury burns,
>
> And into storms the amorous breathings turns;
>
> Then Hope, with heavenward look, and Joy draw near,
>
> While palsied Terror trembles in the rear.

Prologue to *Othello*, as it was acted at the Theatre Royal in Drury Lane on Thursday the 7th of March 1751 by Persons of Distinction for their Diversion. Ll. 21-32.

DAVID HUME, 1754.
(1711-1774)

IF Shakespeare be considered as a MAN, born in a rude age, and educated in the lowest manner, without any instruction, either from the world or from books, he may be regarded as a prodigy. If represented as a POET, capable of furnishing a proper entertainment to a refined or intelligent audience, we must abate much of this eulogy. In his compositions, we regret, that many irregularities, and even absurdities, should so frequently disfigure the animated and passionate scenes intermixed with them; and at the same time, we perhaps admire the more those beauties, on account of their being surrounded with such deformities. A striking peculiarity of sentiment, adapted to a single character, he frequently hits, as it were, by inspiration; but a reasonable propriety of thought he cannot for any time uphold. Nervous and picturesque expressions as well as descriptions abound in him; but it is in vain we look either for purity or simplicity of diction. His total ignorance of all theatrical art and conduct, however material a defect, yet, as it affects the spectator rather than the reader, we can more easily excuse, than that want of taste which often prevails in his productions, and which gives way only by intervals to the irradiations of genius. A great and fertile genius he certainly possessed, and one enriched equally with a tragic and comic vein; but he ought to be cited as a proof, how dangerous it is to rely on these advantages alone for attaining an excellence in the finer arts. And there may even remain a suspicion, that we over-rate, if possible, the greatness of his genius; in the same manner as bodies often appear more gigantic, on account of their being disproportioned and misshapen. He died in 1616, aged fifty-three years.

Jonson possessed all the learning which was wanting to Shakespeare, and wanted all the genius of which the other was possessed. Both of them were equally deficient in taste and elegance, in harmony and correctness. A servile copyist of the ancients, Jonson translated into bad English the beautiful passages of the Greek and Roman authors, without accommodating to the manners of his age and country. His merit has been totally eclipsed by that of Shakespeare, whose rude genius prevailed over the rude art of his contemporary. The English theatre has ever since taken a strong tincture of Shakespeare's spirit and character; and thence it has proceeded, that the nation has undergone from all its neighbours the reproach of barbarism, from which its valuable productions in some parts of learning would otherwise have exempted it.

Appendix to the Reign of James I. History of England from the Invasion of Julius Cæsar to the Revolution in 1688. 1754.

HORACE WALPOLE, EARL OF ORFORD, 1756
(1717-1797)

JOHN and I are just going to Garrick's with a grove of cypresses in our hands, like the Kentish men at the Conquest. He has built a temple to his master Shakespeare, and I am going to adorn the outside, since his modesty would not let me decorate it within, as I proposed, with these mottoes:

> Quod spiro et placeo, si placeo, tuum est.

> That I spirit have and nature,

> That sense breathes in ev'ry feature,

That I please, if please I do,—

Shakespeare,—all I owe to you.

Letter to George Montagu, 14 Oct. 1756. *Letters*, ed. Peter Cunningham, 1857, vol. iii. p. 36.

JOHN ARMSTRONG, 1758
(1709-1779)

SHAKESPEARE, who I will venture to say had the most musical ear of all the English poets, is abundantly irregular in his versification: but his wildest licences seldom hurt the ear; on the contrary, they give his verse a spirit and variety, which prevent its ever cloying. Our modern tragedy-writers, instead of using the advantages of their own languages, seem in general to imitate the monotony of the French versification: and the only licence they ever venture upon, is that poor tame one the supernumerary syllable at the end of a line; which they are apt to manage in such a manner as to give their verse a most ungraceful halt. But it is not want of ear alone which makes our common manufacturers of tragedy so insipidly solemn and so void of harmony: it is want of feeling.

"Of the Versification of English Tragedy." *Works*, 1770, ii. 164-5.

Shakespeare, indeed, without one perfect plan, has perhaps excelled all other dramatic poets as to detached scenes. But he was a wonder!—His deep knowledge of human nature, his prodigious variety of fancy and invention, and of characters drawn with the strongest, truest, and most exquisite strokes, oblige you to forget his most violent irregularities.

Of the Dramatic Unities, *ib.*, p. 242.

WILLIAM MASON, 1759
(1724-1797)

HOW oft I cried, "Oh come, thou tragic queen!

March from thy Greece with firm majestic tread!

Such as when Athens saw thee fill her scene,

When Sophocles thy choral graces led:

Saw thy proud pall its purple length devolve;

Saw thee uplift the glittering dagger high;

Ponder with fixed brow thy deep resolve,

Prepar'd to strike, to triumph, and to die.

Bring then to Britain's plain that choral throng;

Display thy buskin'd pomp, thy golden lyre;

Give her historic forms the soul of song,

And mingle Attic art with Shakespeare's fire."

"Ah, what, fond boy, dost thou presume to claim?"

The Muse replied, "mistaken suppliant, know,

To light in Shakespeare's breast the dazzling flame

Exhausted all Parnassus could bestow.

True, art remains; and if from his bright page

Thy mimic power one vivid beam can seize,

Proceed; and in that best of tasks engage,

Which tends at once to profit, and to please."

Caractacus, 1759.

THOMAS GRAY, 1759
(1716-1771)

FAR from the sun and summer-gale,

In thy green lap [*i.e.* Albion's] was Nature's darling laid,

What time, where lucid Avon strayed,

To him the mighty mother did unveil

Her awful face: The dauntless child

Stretch'd forth his little arms, and smil'd.

This pencil take (she said) whose colours clear

Richly paint the vernal year:

Thine too these golden keys, immortal boy!

This can unlock the gates of Joy;

Of Horror that, and thrilling Fears,

Or ope the sacred source of sympathetic Tears.

The Progress of Poesy. A Pindaric Ode, 1759, iii. 1.

DAVID MALLET, 1759
(1705?-1765)

> PRIDE of his own, and wonder of this age,
>
> Who first created, and yet rules, the Stage,
>
> Bold to design, all powerful to express,
>
> Shakespear each passion drew in every dress:
>
> Great above rule, and imitating none;
>
> Rich without borrowing, nature was his own.
>
> Yet is his sense debas'd by gross alloy:
>
> As gold in mines lies mix'd with dirt and clay.
>
> Now, eagle-wing'd, his heavenward flight he takes;
>
> The big stage thunders, and the soul awakes:
>
> Now, low on earth, a kindred reptile creeps;
>
> Sad Hamlet quibbles, and the hearer sleeps.

Of Verbal Criticism, ll. 47-58. *Works*, 1759, vol. i. p. 21.

EDWARD YOUNG, 1759
(1683-1765)

WHO knows whether Shakespeare might not have thought less, if he had read more? Who knows if he might not have laboured under the load of Jonson's learning, as Enceladus under Ætna? His mighty genius, indeed, though the most mountainous oppression, would have breathed out some of his inextinguishable fire; yet possibly he might not have risen up into that giant, that much more than common man, at which we now gaze with amazement and delight. Perhaps he was as learned as his dramatic province required; for whatever other learning he wanted, he was master of two books unknown to many of the profoundly read, though books which the last conflagration alone can destroy: the book of Nature, and that of Man.

Conjectures on Original Composition. 1759.

MARK AKENSIDE, *c.* 1760
(1721-1770)

"An Inscription."

> O YOUTHS and virgins: O declining eld:
> O pale misfortune's slaves: O ye who dwell
> Unknown with humble quiet; ye who wait
> In courts, or fill the golden seat of kings:
> O sons of sport and pleasure: O thou wretch
> That weep'st for jealous love, or the sore wounds
> Of conscious guilt, or death's rapacious hand
> Which left thee void of hope: O ye who roam
> In exile; ye who through th' embattl'd field
> Seek bright renown; or who for nobler palms
> Contend, the leaders of a public cause;
> Approach: behold this marble. Know ye not
> The features? Hath not oft his faithful tongue
> Told you the fashion of your own estate,
> The secrets of your bosom? Here then round
> His monument with reverence while ye stand,
> Say to each other: "This was Shakespeare's form;
> Who walk'd in every path of human life,
> Felt every passion; and to all mankind
> Doth now, will ever, that experience yield
> Which his own genius only could acquire."

Poetical Works. 1805, ii. pp. 136-7.

ROBERT LLOYD, 1760
(1733-1764)

WHEN Shakespeare leads the mind a dance,

From France to England, hence to France,

Talk not to me of time and place;

I own I'm happy in the chase.

Whether the drama's here or there,

'Tis nature, Shakespeare, everywhere.

The poet's fancy can create,

Contract, enlarge, annihilate,

Bring past and present close together,

In spite of distance, seas, or weather;

And shut up in a single action

What cost whole years in its transaction.

So, ladies at a play or rout,

Can flirt the universe about,

Whose geographical account

Is drawn and pictured on the mount:

Yet when they please, contract the plan,

And shut the world up in a fan.

Shakespeare: An Epistle to Mr. Garrick. 1760, ll. 37-54.

See also Lloyd's *Ode to Genius*, 1760, ll. 1-14.

EDWARD CAPELL, 1760
(1713-1781)

IT is said of the ostrich, that she drops her egg at random, to be disposed of as chance pleases; either brought up to maturity by the sun's kindly warmth, or else crushed by beasts and the feet of passers-by: such, at least, is the account which naturalists have given us of this extraordinary bird; and admitting it for a truth, she is in this a fit emblem of almost every great genius: they conceive and produce with ease those noble issues of human understanding; but incubation, the dull work of putting them correctly upon paper and afterwards publishing, is a task they cannot away with. If the original state of all such authors' writings, even from Homer downward, could be inquired into and known, they would yield proof in abundance of the justness of what is here asserted: but the author now before us shall suffice for them all; being at once the greatest instance of genius in producing noble things, and of negligence in providing for them afterwards.

Preface to *Mr. William Shakespeare, his Comedies, Histories, and Tragedies set out by himself in quarto or by the Players his Fellows in folio, and now faithfully republished from those Editions in ten volumes octavo; with an Introduction, etc.* 1760, vol. i. pp. 1-2.

Of this preface Dr. Johnson remarked: "If the man would have come to me, I would have endeavoured to endow his purpose with words, for as it is, he doth gabble monstrously."—Boswell's *Life of Dr. Johnson*, iii. 251, 2nd ed.

CHARLES CHURCHILL, 1761
(1731-1764)

> IN the first seat, in robe of various dyes,
>
> A noble wildness flashing from his eyes,
>
> Sat Shakespeare.—In one hand a wand he bore,
>
> For mighty wonders fam'd in days of yore;
>
> The other held a globe, which to his will
>
> Obedient turn'd, and own'd the master's skill:
>
> Things of the noblest kind his genius drew,
>
> And look'd through Nature at a single view:
>
> A loose he gave to his unbounded soul,
>
> And taught new lands to rise, new seas to roll;
>
> Call'd into being scenes unknown before,
>
> And, passing Nature's bounds, was something more.

The Rosciad, 1761, l. 259.

WILLIAM WHITEHEAD, 1762
(1715-1785)

BUT chief avoid the boisterous roaring sparks,

The sons of fire!—you'll know them by their marks.

Fond to be heard, they always court a crowd,

And, though 'tis borrow'd nonsense, talk it loud.

One epithet supplies their constant chime,

Damn'd bad, damn'd good, damn'd low, or damn'd sublime.

But most in quick short repartee they shine,

Of local humour; or from plays purloin

Each quaint stale scrap which every subject hits,

Till fools almost imagine, they are wits.

Hear them on Shakespeare! there they foam, they rage!

Yet taste not half the beauties of his page,

Nor see that art, as well as nature strove,

To place him foremost in th' Aonian grove.

For there, there only, where the sisters join,

His genius triumphs, and the work's divine.

Or would ye sift more near these sons of fire,

'Tis Garrick, and not Shakespeare, they admire,

Without his breath, inspiring every thought,

They ne'er perhaps had known what Shakespeare wrote;

Without his eager, his becoming zeal,

To teach them, though they scarce know why, to feel,

A crude unmeaning mass had Jonson been,

And a dead letter Shakespeare's noblest scene.

A Charge to the Poets. 1762, ll. 167-190.

WILLIAM THOMPSON, 1763
(1712?-1766?)

"In Shakespeare's Walk."

BY yon hills, with morning spread,

Lifting up the tufted head,

By those golden waves of corn,

Which the laughing fields adorn,

By the fragrant breath of flowers,

Stealing from the woodbine bowers,

By this thought-inspiring shade,

By the gleamings of the glade,

By the babblings of the brook,

Winding slow in many a crook,

By the rustling of the trees,

By the humming of the bees,

By the woodlark, by the thrush,

Wildly warbling from the bush,

By the fairy's shadowy tread

O'er the cowslip's dewy head,

Father, monarch of the stage,

Glory of Eliza's age,

Shakespeare! deign to lend thy face,

This romantic nook to grace,

Where untaught nature sports alone,

Since thou and nature are but one.

Garden Inscriptions. Poetical Calendar, 1763. First reprinted in Anderson's *Poets of Great Britain,* 1794, vol. x. p. 993.

SAMUEL JOHNSON, 1765
(1709-1784)

THE work of a correct and regular writer is a garden accurately formed and diligently planted, varied with shades, and scented with flowers; the composition of Shakespeare is a forest, in which oaks extend their branches, and pines tower in the air, interspersed sometimes with weeds and brambles, and sometimes giving shelter to myrtles and to roses; filling the eye with awful pomp, and gratifying the mind with endless diversity. Other poets display cabinets of precious rarities, minutely finished, wrought into shape, and polished into brightness. Shakespeare opens a mine which contains gold and diamonds in unexhaustible plenty, though clouded by incrustations, debased by impurities, and mingled with a mass of meaner minerals.

Preface to Shakespeare's *Works*. 1765.

In *The Rambler*, No. 156 (14 Sept. 1751), Johnson wrote: "Instead of vindicating tragi-comedy by the success of Shakespeare, we ought perhaps to pay new honours to that transcendent and unbounded genius that could preside over the passions in sport; who, to actuate the affections, needed not the slow gradation of common means, but could fill the heart with instantaneous jollity or sorrow, and vary our disposition as he changed his scenes. Perhaps the effects even of Shakespeare's poetry might have been greater, had he not counteracted himself; and we might have been more interested in the distresses of his heroes, had we not been so frequently diverted by the jokes of his buffoons."

GEORGE KEATE, 1768
(1729-1797)

> YES! jealous wits may still for empire strive,
>
> Still keep the flames of critick rage alive:
>
> Our Shakespeare yet shall all his rights maintain,
>
> And crown the triumphs of Eliza's reign,
>
> Above control, above each classick rule,
>
> His tutress Nature, and the World his school.
>
> On daring pinions borne, to him was given
>
> Th' aerial range of Fancy's brightest Heaven,
>
> To bid rapt thought o'er noblest heights aspire,
>
> And wake each passion with a Muse of Fire.

Revere his genius—to the dead be just,

And spare the laurels, that o'ershade the dust.

Low sleeps the bard, *in cold obstruction laid,*

Nor asks the chaplet from a rival's head.

O'er the dear vault, Ambition's utmost bound,

Unheard shall Fame her airy trumpet sound!

Unheard alike, nor grief nor transport raise,

Thy blast of censure, or thy note of praise!

As Raphael's own creation grac'd his hearse,

And sham'd the pomp of ostentatious verse,

Shall Shakespeare's honours by himself be paid,

And Nature perish ere his pictures fade.

Ferney: An Epistle to Monsr. De Voltaire. 1768. *Poetical Works,* 1781, pp. 136-7.

Raphael's Own Creation:—The TRANSFIGURATION, that well-known picture of RAPHAEL, was carried before his body to the grave, doing more real honour to his memory than either his epitaph in the Pantheon, the famous distich of CARDINAL BEMBO, or all the other adulatory verses written on the same occasion.—KEATE.

DAVID GARRICK, 1769
(1717-1779)

"Warwickshire."

YE *Warwickshire* lads, and ye lasses,

See what at our Jubilee passes;

Come revel away, rejoice and be glad;

For the lad of all lads, was a *Warwickshire* lad,

Warwickshire lad,

All be glad;

For the lad of all lads, was a *Warwickshire* lad.

Be proud of the charms of your county,

Where Nature has lavish'd her bounty;

Where much she has giv'n, and some to be spar'd;

For the bard of all bards, was a *Warwickshire* bard,

Warwickshire bard,

Never pair'd;

For the bard of all bards, was a *Warwickshire* bard.

Each shire has its different pleasures,

Each shire has its different treasures;

But to rare *Warwickshire*, all must submit;

For the wit of all wits, was a *Warwickshire* wit,

Warwickshire wit,

How he writ!

For the wit of all wits, was a *Warwickshire* wit.

Old Ben, Thomas Otway, John Dryden,

And half a score more we take pride in;

Of famous Will Congreve, we boast too the skill;

But the Will of all Wills, was *Warwickshire* Will,

Warwickshire Will,

Matchless still;

For the Will of all Wills, was a *Warwickshire* Will.

Our Shakespeare compar'd is to no man—

Nor Frenchman, nor Grecian, nor Roman;

Their swans are all geese, to the Avon's sweet swan;

And the man of all men, was a *Warwickshire* man,

Warwickshire man,

Avon's swan;

And the man of all men, was a *Warwickshire* man.

As ven'son is very inviting,

To steal it our bard took delight in.

To make his friends merry he never was lag;

And the wag of all wags, was a *Warwickshire* wag,

Warwickshire wag,

Ever brag;

For the wag of all wags, was a *Warwickshire* wag.

There never was seen such a creature,

Of all she was worth, he robbed Nature;

He took all her smiles, and he took all her grief;

And the thief of all thieves, was a *Warwickshire* thief.

Warwickshire thief,

He's the chief;

For the thief of all thieves, was a *Warwickshire* chief.

"Warwickshire: a Song." *Shakespeare's Garland. Being a Collection of New Songs, Ballads, Roundelays, Catches, Glees, Comic Serenades, etc., performed at the Jubilee at Stratford-upon-Avon.* 1769, p. 2.

ANONYMOUS, 1769

"To the Immortal Memory of Shakespeare."

IMMORTAL be his name,

His memory, his fame!

Nature and her works we see,

Matchless Shakespeare, full in thee!

Join'd by everlasting ties,

Shakespeare but with Nature dies.

Immortal be his Name,

His memory, his fame!

Shakespeare's Garland. Being a Collection of New Songs, Ballads, etc., performed at the Jubilee at Stratford-upon-Avon. 1769, p. 15.

WILLIAM RICHARDSON, 1774
(1743-1814)

NO writer has hitherto appeared who possesses in a more eminent degree than Shakespeare, the power of imitating the passions. All of them seem familiar to him; the boisterous no less than the gentle; the benign no less than the malignant. There are several writers, as there are many players, who are successful in imitating some particular passions, but who appear stiff, awkward, and unnatural, in the expression of others. Some are capable of exhibiting very striking representations of resolute and intrepid natures, but cannot so easily bend themselves to those that are softer and more complacent. Others, again, seem full of amiable affection and tenderness, but cannot exalt themselves to the boldness of the hero, or magnanimity of the patriot. The genius of Shakespeare is unlimited. Possessing extreme sensibility, and uncommonly susceptible, he is the Proteus of the drama; he changes himself into every character, and enters easily into every condition of human nature.

Many dramatic writers of different ages are capable, occasionally, of breaking out, with great fervour of genius, in the natural language of strong emotion. No writer of antiquity is more distinguished for abilities of this kind than Euripides. His whole heart and soul seem torn and agitated by the force of the passion he imitates. He ceases to be Euripides; he is Medea; he is Orestes. Shakespeare, however, is most eminently distinguished, not only by these occasional sallies, but by imitating the passion in all its aspects, by pursuing it through all its windings and labyrinths, by moderating or accelerating its impetuosity according to the influence of other principles and of external events, and finally by combining it in a judicious manner with other passions and propensities, or by setting it aptly in opposition. He thus unites the two essential powers of dramatic invention, that of forming characters; and that of imitating in their natural expressions, the passions and affections of which they are composed.

A Philosophical Analysis and Illustration of some of Shakespeare's remarkable Characters. 1774. Introduction, pp. 39-42.

WILLIAM JULIUS MICKLE, 1775
(1735-1788)

WHEN Heaven decreed to soothe the feuds that tore

The wolf-eyed barons, whose unletter'd rage

Spurn'd the fair muse, Heaven bade on Avon's shore

A Shakespeare rise, and soothe the barbarous age:

A Shakespeare rose; the barbarous heats assuage.

At distance due how many bards attend!

Enlarged and liberal from the narrow cage

Of blinded zeal, new manners wide extend,

And o'er the generous breast the dews of heaven descend.

Introduction to *The Lusiad, or the Discovery of India. An Epic Poem.* Translated, 1775.

WILLIAM HAYLEY, 1777
(1745-1820)

WHEN mighty Shakespeare to thy judging eye

Presents that magic glass whose ample round

Reflects each figure in Creation's bound,

And pours, in floods of supernatural light,

Fancy's bright beings on the charmed sight,

This chief enchanter of the willing breast

Will teach thee all the magic he possessed.

Placed in his circle, mark in colours true

Each brilliant being that he calls to view:

Wrapt in the gloomy storm, or robed in light,

His weird sister or his fairy sprite.

Boldly o'erleaping, in the great design,

The bounds of nature, with a guide divine.

A Poetic Epistle to an Eminent Painter [George Romney]. 2nd edition, 1779. Part II. ll. 472-84.

THOMAS WARTON, 1777
(1728-1790)

AVON, thy rural view, thy pastures wild,
The willows that o'erhang thy twilight edge,
Their boughs entangling with the embattled sedge;
Thy brink with watery foliage quaintly fring'd,
Thy surface with reflected verdure ting'd;
Soothe me with many a pensive pleasure mild.
But while I muse, that here the bard divine,
Whose sacred dust yon high arch'd aisles enclose,
Where the tall windows rise in stately rows
Above the embowering shade,
Here first, at Fancy's fairy-circled shrine,
Of daisies pied his infant offering made;
Here playful yet, in stripling years unripe,
Fram'd of thy reeds a shrill and artless pipe:
Sudden thy beauties, Avon, all are fled,
As at the waving of some magic wand;
An holy trance my charmed spirit wings,
And awful shapes of warriors and of kings
People the busy mead,
Like spectres swarming to the wizard's hall;
And slowly pace, and point with trembling hand
The wounds ill-cover'd with the purple pall.
Before me Pity seems to stand
A weeping mourner, smote with anguish sore,
To see Misfortune rend in frantic mood
His robe, with regal woes embroider'd o'er.

Pale Terror leads the visionary band,

And sternly shakes his sceptre dropping blood.

"Monody written near Stratford-upon-Avon." *Miscellaneous Odes.* 1777.

ANNA SEWARD, **BEFORE** 1782
(1747-1809)

"On Shakespeare's Monument at Stratford-upon-Avon."

> GREAT Homer's birth sev'n rival cities claim,
>
> Too mighty such monopoly of Fame;
>
> Yet not to birth alone did Homer owe
>
> His wondrous worth; what Egypt could bestow,
>
> With all the schools of Greece and Asia join'd,
>
> Enlarg'd th' immense expansion of his mind.
>
> Nor yet unrival'd the Mæonian strain,
>
> The British Eagle and the Mantuan Swan
>
> Tow'r equal heights. But happier Stratford, thou
>
> With incontested laurels deck thy brow:
>
> Thy bard was thine *unschool'd*, and from thee brought
>
> More than all Egypt, Greece, or Asia taught.
>
> Not Homer's self such matchless honours won;
>
> The Greek has rivals, but thy Shakespeare none.

Dodsley's *Collection of Poems by Several Hands.* 1782, ii. p. 315.

"The British Eagle," *i.e.* Milton.

WILLIAM LISLE BOWLES, 1794
(1762-1850)

"On Shakespeare."

> O SOVEREIGN master, who with lovely state

Dost rule as in some isle's enchanted land,

On whom soft airs and shadowy spirits wait,

Whilst scenes of faerie bloom at thy command!

On thy wild shores forgetful could I lie,

And list, till earth dissolved, to thy sweet minstrelsy!

Called by thy magic from the hoary deep,

Aërial forms should in bright troops ascend,

And then a wondrous masque before me sweep;

While sounds *that the earth owned not*, seem to blend

Their stealing melodies, that when the strain

Ceased, *I should weep, and would so dream again!*

The charm is wound: I see an aged form,

In white robes, on the winding sea-shore stand;

O'er the careering surge he waves his wand:

Upon the black rock bursts the bidden storm.

Now from bright opening clouds I hear a lay,

Come to these yellow sands, fair stranger, come away.

Saw ye pass by the weird sisters pale?

Marked ye the lowering castle on the heath?

Hark! hark! is the deed done? the deed of death!

The deed is done—hail, king of Scotland, hail!

I see no more;—to many a fearful sound

The bloody cauldron sinks, and all is dark around.

Pity! touch the trembling strings,

A maid, a beauteous maniac, wildly sings:

"They laid him in the ground so cold,

Upon his breast the earth is thrown;

High is heaped the grassy mould,

Oh! he is dead and gone.

The winds of the winter blow o'er his cold breast,

But pleasant shall be his rest."

The song is ceased. Ah! who, pale shade, art thou,

Sad raving to the rude tempestuous night?

Sure thou hast had much wrong, so stern thy brow;

So piteous thou dost tear thy tresses white;

So wildly thou dost cry, *"Blow, bitter wind,*

Ye elements, I call not YOU *unkind."*

Beneath the shade of nodding branches grey,

And rude romantic woods, and glens forlorn,

The merry hunters wear the hours away;

Rings the deep forest to the joyous horn!

Joyous to all, but him who with sad look

Hangs idly musing by the brawling brook.

But mark the merry elves of fairy land!

To the high moon's gleamy glance,

They with shadowy morris dance;

Soft music dies along the desert sand;

Soon at peep of cold-eyed day

Soon the numerous lights decay;

Merrily, now merrily,

After the dewy moon they fly.

Let rosy laughter now advance,

And wit with sparkling eye,

Where quaint powers lurking lie

Bright fancy, the queen of the revels, shall dance,

And point to the frolicsome train

And antic forms that flit unnumbered o'er the plain.

O sovereign master! at whose sole command

We start with terror, or with pity weep;

O! where is now thy all-creating wand?

Buried ten thousand fathoms in the deep.

The staff is broke, the powerful spell is fled,

And never earthly guest shall in thy circle tread.

Sonnets, with other Poems. 3rd edition. 1794, pp. 67-70.

This poem appears in later editions of Bowle's sonnets in a different form. Stanza 9 is omitted, and the remaining stanzas are arranged thus: 1, 2, 6, 7, 8, 3, 4, 5, 10:

"Come to these yellow sands." Ferdinand. See *The Tempest.*

"The weird sisters." See *Macbeth.*

"A beauteous maniac." Ophelia. See *Hamlet.*

"Blow, bitter wind." See *King Lear.*

"Him, who with sad look." Jacques. See *As You Like It.*

"Elves of fairy land." See *Midsummer Night's Dream.*

THE THIRD PERIOD
NINETEENTH CENTURY

WILLIAM WORDSWORTH, 1802
(1770-1850)

> IT is not to be thought of that the flood
>
> Of British freedom, which, to the open sea
>
> Of the world's praise, from dark antiquity
>
> Hath flowed "with pomp of waters unwithstood,"
>
> Roused though it be full often to a mood
>
> Which spurns the check of salutary bands,

That this most famous stream in bogs and sands

Should perish; and to evil and to good

Be lost for ever. In our halls is hung

Armoury of the invincible knights of old:

We must be free or die, who speak the tongue

That Shakspeare spake; the faith and morals hold

Which Milton held. In everything we are sprung

Of Earth's first blood, have titles manifold.

"Sonnets dedicated to Liberty." *Poems.* 1807.

FELICIA DOROTHEA HEMANS, 1804
(1793-1835)

"Shakespeare."

I LOVE to rove o'er history's page,

Recall the hero and the sage;

Revive the actions of the dead,

And memory of ages fled:

Yet it yields me greater pleasure

To read the poet's pleasing measure.

Led by Shakespeare, bard inspired,

The bosom's energies are fired;

We learn to shed the generous tear

O'er poor Ophelia's sacred bier;

To love the merry moonlit scene,

With fairy elves in valleys green;

Or borne on fancy's heavenly wings,

To listen while sweet Ariel sings.

How sweet the native wood notes wild

Of him, the Muse's favourite child!

Of him whose magic lays impart

Each various feeling to the heart.

Poems. By Felicia Dorothea Browne, 1808, p. 48.

One of Mrs. Hemans' earliest tastes—relates her sister in her *Memoirs*—was a passion for Shakespeare, which she read as her choicest recreation at six years old. The above lines were written when she was eleven years of age.

SIR WALTER SCOTT, 1814
(1771-1832)

THE English stage might be considered as equally without rule and without model when Shakespeare arose. The effect of the genius of an individual upon the taste of a nation is mighty; but that genius, in its turn, is formed according to the opinions prevalent at the period when it comes into existence. Such was the case with Shakespeare. With an education more extensive, and a taste refined by the classical models, it is probable that he also, in admiration of the ancient drama, might have mistaken the form for the essence, and subscribed to those rules which had produced such masterpieces of art. Fortunately for the full exertion of a genius as comprehensive and versatile, as intense and powerful, Shakespeare had no access to any models of which the commanding merit might have controlled and limited his own exertions. He followed the path which a nameless crowd of obscure writers had trodden before him; but he moved in it with the grace and majestic step of a being of a superior order, and vindicated for ever the British theatre from a pedantic restriction to classical rule. Nothing went before Shakespeare which in any respect was fit to fix and stamp the character of a national drama; and certainly no one will succeed him, capable of establishing by mere authority, a form more restricted than that which Shakespeare used.

Article on "Drama," *Encyclopædia Britannica.* 4th ed. 1814. 6th ed. vol. viii. p. 157.

SAMUEL TAYLOR COLERIDGE, 1817
(1772-1834)

NO man was ever yet a great poet, without being at the same time a profound philosopher. For poetry is the blossom and the fragrancy of all human knowledge, human thoughts, human passions, emotions, language. In Shakespeare's POEMS, the creative power, and the intellectual energy, wrestle as in a war embrace. Each in its excess of strength seems to threaten the extinction of the other. At length in the DRAMA they were reconciled, and fought each with its shield before the breast of the other. Or, like two rapid streams, that at their first meeting within narrow and rocky banks, mutually strive to repel each other, and intermix reluctantly and in tumult; but soon finding a wider channel and more yielding shores, blend, and dilate, and flow on in one current and with one voice. The "Venus and Adonis" did not, perhaps, allow the display of the deeper passions. But the story of Lucretia seems to favour, and even demand their intensest workings. And yet we find in *Shakespeare's* management of the tale, neither pathos, nor any other *dramatic* quality. There is the same minute and faithful imagery as in the former poem, in the same vivid colours, inspirited by the same impetuous vigour of thought, and diverging and contracting with the same activity of the assimilative and of the modifying faculties; and with a yet larger display, a yet wider range of knowledge and reflection; and, lastly, with the same perfect dominion, often *domination*, over the whole world of language. What then shall we say? even this: that—

Shakespeare, no mere child of nature; no automaton of genius; no passive vehicle of inspiration possessed by the spirit, not possessing it; first studied patiently, meditated deeply, understood minutely, till knowledge, become habitual and intuitive, wedded itself to his habitual feelings, and at length gave birth to that stupendous power, by which he stands alone, with no equal or second in his own class; to that power, which seated him on one of the two glory-smitten summits of the poetic mountain, with Milton as his compeer, not rival. While the former darts himself forth, and passes into all the forms of human character and passion, to one Proteus of the fire and the flood; the other attracts all forms and things to himself, in the unity of his own IDEAL. All things and modes of action shape themselves anew in the being of MILTON; while SHAKESPEARE becomes all things, yet for ever remaining himself. O what great men hast thou not produced, England! my country!

Biographia Literaria. 1817, chap. xv.

The following is from Coleridge's *Literary Remains*, ed. Henry Nelson Coleridge, 1867, ii. pp. 68-69:—I greatly dislike beauties and selections in general; but as proof positive of his unrivalled excellence, I should like to try Shakespeare by this criterion. Make out your amplest catalogue of all the human faculties, as reason or the moral law, the will, the feeling of the coincidence of the two (a feeling *sui generis et demonstratio demonstrationum*) called the conscience, the understanding or prudence, wit, fancy, imagination, judgment,—and then of the objects on which these are to be employed, as the beauties, the terrors, and the seeming caprices of nature, the realities and the capabilities, that is, the actual and the ideal, of the human mind, conceived as an individual or as a social being, as in innocence or in guilt, in a play-paradise, or in a war-field of temptation; and then compare with Shakespeare under each of these heads all or any of the writers in prose and verse that have ever lived! Who, that is competent to judge, doubts the result? And ask your own hearts,—ask your own common-sense—to conceive the possibility of this man being—I say not, the drunken savage of that wretched sciolist, whom Frenchmen, to their shame, have honoured before their elder and better worthies,—but the anomalous, the wild, the irregular, genius of our daily criticism! What! are we to have miracles in sport? Or, I speak reverently, does God choose idiots by whom to convey divine truths to man?

For a passage on Shakespeare as a "philosophical aristocrat" who "never promulgates any party tenets," see "Notes on the *Tempest*."

FRANCIS LORD JEFFREY, 1817
(1773-1850)

MORE full of wisdom and ridicule and sagacity, than all the moralists and satirists that ever existed—he [Shakespeare] is more wild, airy and inventive, and more pathetic and fantastic, than all the poets of all regions and ages of the world:—and has all those elements so happily mixed up in him, and bears his high faculties so temperately, that the most severe reader cannot complain of him for want of strength or of reason—nor the most sensitive for defect of ornament or ingenuity. Every thing in him is in unmeasured abundance, and unequalled perfection—but everything so balanced and kept in subordination, as not to jostle or disturb or take the place of another. The most exquisite poetical conceptions, images, and descriptions are given with such brevity, and introduced with such skill, as merely to adorn, without loading the sense they accompany. Although his sails are purple and perfumed, and his prow of beaten gold, they waft him on his voyage, not less, but more rapidly and directly than if they had been composed of baser materials. All his excellences, like those of Nature herself, are thrown out together; and instead of interfering with, support and recommend each other. His flowers are not tied up in garlands, nor his fruits crushed into baskets—but spring living from the soil, in all the dew and freshness of youth; while the graceful foliage in which they lurk, and the ample branches, the rough and vigorous stem, and the wide-spreading roots on which they depend, are present along with them, and share, in their places, the equal care of their Creator.

The Edinburgh Review, August 1817. Art. IX. "Characters of Shakespeare's Plays, by William Hazlitt."
Vol. xxviii. p. 474.

WILLIAM HAZLITT, 1818
(1778-1830)

THE striking peculiarity of Shakespeare's mind was its generic quality, its power of communication with all other minds—so that it contained a universe of thought and feeling within itself, and had no one peculiar bias, or exclusive excellence more than another. He was just like any other man, but that he was like all other men. He was the least of an egotist that it was possible to be. He was nothing in himself; but he was all that others were, or that they could become. He not only had in himself the germs of every faculty and feeling, but he could follow them by anticipation, intuitively, into all their conceivable ramifications, through every change of fortune or conflict of passion, or turn of thought. He had "a mind reflecting ages past," and present:—All the people that ever lived are there. There was no respect of persons with him. His genius alone shone equally on the evil and on the good, on the wise and the foolish, the monarch and the beggar: "All corners of the earth, kings, queens, and states, maids, matrons, nay, the secrets of the grave," are hardly hid from his searching glance. He was like the genius of humanity, changing places with all of us at pleasure, and playing with our purposes as with his own. He turned the globe round for his amusement, and surveyed the generations of men, and the individuals as they passed, with their different concerns, passions, follies, vices, virtues, actions, and motives—as well those that they knew, as those which they did not know, or acknowledge to themselves. The dreams of childhood, the ravings of despair, were the toys of his fancy. Airy beings waited at his call, and came at his bidding. Harmless fairies nodded to him, and did him curtesies: and the night-hag bestrode the blast at the command of "his so potent art." The world of spirits lay open to him, like the world of real men and women: and there is the same truth in his delineations of the one as of the other; for if the preternatural characters he describes could be supposed to exist, they would speak, and feel, and act, as he makes them. He had only to think of any thing in order to become that thing, with all the circumstances belonging to it. When he conceived of a character, whether real or imaginary, he not only entered into all its thoughts and feelings, but seemed instantly, and as if by touching a secret spring, to be surrounded with all the same objects, "subject to the same skyey influences," the same local, outward, and unforeseen accidents which would occur in reality.

"On Shakespeare and Milton," *Lectures on The English Poets*. 1818, pp. 91-3.

For a comment on this passage by William Minto, see p. 189.

The following occurs in Hazlitt's essay "On Dryden and Pope" (*ib.*, pp. 137-38):—The poet of nature is one who, from the elements of beauty, of power, and of passion in his own breast, sympathises with whatever is beautiful, and grand, and impassioned in nature, in its simple majesty, in its immediate appeal to the senses, to the thoughts and hearts of all men; so that the poet of nature, by the truth, and depth, and harmony of his mind, may be said to hold communion with the very soul of nature; to be identified with and to foreknow and to record the feelings of all men at all times and places, as they are liable to the same impressions; and to exert the same power over the minds of his readers, that nature does. He sees things in their eternal beauty, for he sees them as they are; he feels them in their universal interest, for he feels them as they affect the first principles of his and our common nature. Such was Homer, such was Shakespeare, whose works will last as long as nature, because they are a copy of the indestructible forms and everlasting impulses of nature, welling out from the bosom as from a perennial spring, or stamped upon the senses by the hand of their maker. The power of the imagination in them, is the representative power of all nature. It has its centre in the human soul, and makes the circuit of the universe.

See also *The Round Table*, 1817—"On Posthumous Fame—whether Shakespeare was influenced by a love of it."

JOHN KEATS, *c.* 1818
(1795-1821)

THE genius of Shakespeare was an innate universality—wherefore he had the utmost achievement of human intellect prostrate beneath his indolent and kingly gaze. He could do easily Man's utmost. His plans of tasks to come were not of this world—if what he purposed to do hereafter would not in his own Idea "answer the aim," how tremendous must have been his Conception of Ultimates!

Note on Troilus and Cressida, I. iii. Marginalia from the Shakespeare Folio of 1808. (*Works*, ed. H. Buxton Forman. 1901, iii. p. 254.)

c. 1818

"*Sonnet on sitting down to read* KING LEAR *once again.*"

O GOLDEN-TONGUED Romance, with serene lute!

Fair-plumed Syren, Queen of far-away!

Leave melodising on this wintry day,

Shut up thine olden pages, and be mute:

Adieu! for, once again, the fierce dispute

Betwixt damnation and impassion'd clay

Must I burn through; once more humbly assay

The bitter-sweet of this Shakespearian fruit:

Chief Poet! and ye clouds of Albion,

Begetters of our deep eternal theme!

When through the old oak Forest I am gone,

Let me not wander in a barren dream,

But, when I am consumed in the fire,

Give me new Phœnix wings to fly at my desire.

Life, Letters, and Literary Remains of John Keats, edited by Richard Monckton Milnes. Vol. i. p. 96.

JOHN WILSON, 1819
(1785-1854)

SHAKESPEARE is of no age. He speaks a language which thrills in our blood in spite of the separation of two hundred years. His thoughts, passions, feelings, strains of fancy, all are of this day, as they were of his own—and his genius may be contemporary with the mind of every generation for a thousand years to come. He, above all poets, looked upon man, and lived for mankind. His genius, universal in intellect, could find, in no more bounded circumference, its proper sphere. It could not bear exclusion from any part of human existence. Whatever in nature and life was given to man, was given in contemplation and poetry to him also, and over the undimmed mirror of his mind passed all the shadows of our mortal world. Look through his plays and tell what form of existence, what quality of spirit, he is most skilful to delineate. Which of all the manifold beings he has drawn, lives before our thoughts, our eyes, in most unpictured reality? Is it Othello, Shylock, Falstaff, Lear, the wife of Macbeth, Imogen, Hamlet, Ariel? In none of the other great dramatists do we see anything like a perfected art. In their works, everything, it is true, exists in some shape or other, which can be required in a drama taking for its interest the absolute interest of human life and nature; but, after all, may not the very best of their works be looked on as sublime masses of chaotic confusion, through which the elements of our moral being appear? It was Shakespeare, the most unlearned of all our writers, who first exhibited on the stage perfect models, perfect images of all human characters, and all human events. We cannot conceive any skill that could from his great characters remove any defect, or add to their perfect composition. Except in him, we look in vain for the entire fulness, the self-consistency, and self-completeness of perfect art.

"A few words on Shakespeare, May 1819." *Essays Critical and Imaginative.* 1866, vol. iii. pp. 420-21.

CHARLES SPRAGUE, 1824
(1791-1875)

WHO now shall grace the glowing throne,

Where, all unrivall'd, all alone,

Bold Shakespeare sat, and look'd creation through,

The minstrel monarch of the worlds he drew?

That throne is cold—that lyre in death unstrung,

On whose proud note delighted Wonder hung.

Yet old Oblivion, as in wrath he sweeps,

One spot shall spare—the grave where Shakespeare sleeps.

Rulers and ruled in common gloom may lie,

But Nature's laureate bards shall never die.

Art's chisell'd boast and glory's trophied shore

Must live in numbers or can live no more.

While sculptured Jove some nameless waste may claim,

Still roars the Olympic car in Pindar's fame:

Troy's doubtful walls, in ashes pass'd away,

Yet frown on Greece in Homer's deathless lay;

Rome, slowly sinking in her crumbling fanes,

Stands all immortal in her Maro's strains;

So, too, yon giant empress of the isles,

On whose broad sway the sun for ever smiles,

To Time's unsparing rage one day must bend,

And all her triumphs in her Shakespeare end!

O thou! to whose creative power

We dedicate the festal hour,

While Grace and Goodness round the altar stand,

Learning's anointed train, and Beauty's rose-lipp'd band—

Realms yet unborn, in accents now unknown,

Thy song shall learn, and bless it for their own.

Deep in the west, as Independence roves,

His banners planting round the land he loves,

Where Nature sleeps in Eden's infant grace,

In Time's full hour shall spring a glorious race:

Thy name, thy verse, thy language shall they bear,

And deck for thee the vaulted temple there.

Our Roman-hearted fathers broke

Thy parent empire's galling yoke,

But thou, harmonious monarch of the mind,

Around their sons a gentler chain shall bind;

Still o'er our land shall Albion's sceptre wave,

And what her mighty Lion lost, her mightier Swan shall save.

Prize Ode recited at the representation of the Shakespeare Jubilee, Boston, February 13, 1824.

CHARLES LAMB, 1824
(1775-1834)

IN "sad civility" once Garrick sate

To see a play, mangled in form and state;

Plebeian Shakespeare must the words supply,—

The actors all were fools—of Quality.

The scenes—the dresses—were above rebuke;—

Scarce a performer there below a Duke.

He sate, and mused how in his Shakespeare's mind

The idea of old nobility enshrined

Should thence a grace and a refinement have

Which passed these living Nobles to conceive—

Who with such apish, base gesticulation,

Remnants of starts, and dregs of playhouse passion,

So foul belied their great forefathers' fashion!

He saw—and true nobility confessed

Less in the high-born blood, than lowly poet's breast.

"Epilogue to an amateur Performance of Richard II.," ll. 10-24. *Works of Charles and Mary Lamb.* Ed. E. V. Lucas, 1903-4. Vol. v. p. 128.

JULIUS CHARLES HARE, 1827
(1795-1855)

SHAKESPEARE "glances from heaven to earth, from earth to heaven." All Nature ministers to him, as gladly as a mother to her child. Whether he wishes her to tune her myriad-voiced organ to Romeo's love, or to Miranda's innocence, or to Perdita's simplicity, or to Rosalind's playfulness, or to the sports of the Fairies, or to Timon's misanthropy, or to Macbeth's desolating ambition, or to Lear's heart-broken frenzy—he has only to ask, and she puts on every feeling and every passion with which he desires to invest her.

No poet comes near Shakespeare in the number of bosom lines,—of lines that we may cherish in our bosoms, and that seem almost as if they had grown there,—of lines that, like bosom friends, are ever at hand to comfort, counsel, and gladden us, under all the vicissitudes of life,—of lines that, according to Bacon's expression, "come home to our business and bosoms," and open the door for us to look in, and see what is nestling and brooding there.

Guesses at Truth. 1827.

JAMES HOGG, 1831
(1770-1835)

"To the Genius of Shakespeare."

   SPIRIT all limitless,

   Where is thy dwelling-place?

   Spirit of him whose high name we revere,

   Come on thy seraph wings,

   Come from thy wanderings,

   And smile on thy votaries, who sigh for thee here!

   Come, O thou spark divine,

   Rise from thy hallowed shrine;

   Here in the windings of Forth thou shalt see

   Hearts true to nature's call

   Spirits congenial,

   Proud of their country, yet bowing to thee.

   Here with rapt heart and tongue,

   While our fond minds were young,

   Oft thy bold numbers we poured in our mirth;

   Now in our hall for aye

   This shall be holiday,

   Bard of all Nature, to honour thy birth.

   Whether thou tremblest o'er

   Green grave of Elsinore,

   Stayest o'er the hill of Dunsinnan to hover,

   Bosworth, or Shrewsbury,

   Egypt or Philippi;

Come from thy roamings the universe over.

Whether thou journey'st far
On by the morning star,
Dream'st on the shadowy brows of the moon,
Or linger'st in fairyland,
'Mid lovely elves to stand,
Singing thy carols unearthly and boon;—

Here thou art called upon,
Come thou to Caledon!
Come to the land of the ardent and free!
The land of the love recess,
Mountain and wilderness,
This is the land, thou wild meteor, for thee!

Oh, never since time had birth,
Rose from the pregnant earth
Gems such as late have in Scotia sprung;—
Gems that in future day,
When ages pass away,
Like thee shall be honoured, like thee shall be sung!

Then here, by the sounding sea,
Forest, and greenwood tree,
Here to solicit thee cease shall we never:
Yes, thou effulgence bright,
Here must thy flame relight,
Or vanish from Nature for ever and ever!

Songs. By the Ettrick Shepherd. Now first collected. 1831, p. 304.

CHARLES LAMB, 1833
(1775-1834)

I AM jealous of the combination of the sister arts. Let them sparkle apart. What injury (short of the theatres) did Boydell's Shakespeare Gallery do me with Shakespeare?—to have Opie's Shakespeare, Northcote's Shakespeare, light-headed Fuseli's Shakespeare, heavy-headed Romney's Shakespeare, wooden-headed West's Shakespeare (though he did the best in "Lear"), deaf-headed Reynolds's Shakespeare, instead of my, and everybody's Shakespeare. To be tied down to an authentic face of Juliet! To have Imogen's portrait! To confine the illimitable!

Letter to Samuel Rogers, December 21, 1833. *Works of Charles and Mary Lamb*. Ed. E. V. Lucas, 1903-4. Vol. vii.

HARTLEY COLERIDGE, 1833
(1796-1849)

"To Shakespeare."

> THE soul of man is larger than the sky,
>
> Deeper than ocean, or the abysmal dark
>
> Of the unfathom'd centre. Like that Ark,
>
> Which in its sacred hold uplifted high,
>
> O'er the drown'd hills, the human family,
>
> And stock reserved of every living kind,
>
> So in the compass of the single mind
>
> The seeds and pregnant forms in essence lie,
>
> That make all worlds. Great Poet, 'twas thy art
>
> To know thyself, and in thyself to be
>
> Whate'er love, hate, ambition, destiny,
>
> Or the firm, fatal purpose of the heart,
>
> Can make of Man. Yet thou wert still the same,
>
> Serene of thought, unhurt by thy own flame.

Poems. Sonnet XXVIII. 1833, p. 28.

THOMAS DE QUINCEY, 1838
(1785-1859)

IN the great world of woman, as the interpreter of the shifting phases and the lunar varieties of that mighty changeable planet, that lovely satellite of man, Shakespeare stands not the first only, not the original only, but is yet the sole authentic oracle of truth. Woman, therefore, the beauty of the female mind, *this* is one great field of his power. The supernatural world, the world of apparitions, *that* is another. . . . In all Christendom, who, let us ask, who, who but Shakespeare has found the power for effectually working this mysterious mode of being?

....

A third fund of Shakespeare's peculiar power lies in his teeming fertility of fine thoughts and sentiments. From his works alone might be gathered a golden bead-roll of thoughts, the deepest, subtilest, most pathetic, and yet most catholic and universally intelligible; the most characteristic, also, and appropriate to the particular person, the situation, and the case, yet, at the same time, applicable to the circumstances of every human being, under all the accidents of life, and all vicissitudes of fortune. But this subject offers so vast a field of observation, it being so eminently the prerogative of Shakespeare to have thought more finely and more extensively than all other poets combined, that we cannot wrong the dignity of such a theme by doing more, in our narrow limits, than simply noticing it as one of the emblazonries upon Shakespeare's shield.

Fourthly, we shall indicate (and, as in the last case, *barely* indicate, without attempting in so vast a field to offer any adequate illustrations) one mode of Shakespeare's dramatic excellence, which hitherto has not attracted any special or separate notice. We allude to the forms of life, and natural human passion, as apparent in the structure of his dialogue. Among the many defects and infirmities of the French and of the Italian drama, indeed, we may say of the Greek, the dialogue proceeds always by independent speeches, replying indeed to each other, but never modified in its several terminal forms immediately preceding. Now, in Shakespeare, who first set an example of that most important innovation, in all his impassioned dialogues, each reply or rejoinder seems the mere rebound of the previous speech. Every form of natural interruption, breaking through the restraints of ceremony under the impulses of tempestuous passion; every form of hasty interrogative, ardent reiteration when a question has been evaded; every form of scornful repetition of the hostile words; every impatient continuation of the hostile statement; in short, all modes and formulæ by which anger, hurry, fretfulness, scorn, impatience, or excitement under any movement whatever, can disturb or modify or dislocate the formal bookish style of commencement,—these are as rife in Shakespeare's dialogue as in life itself; and how much vivacity, how profound a verisimilitude, they add to the scenic effect as an imitation of human passion and real life, we need not say. A volume might be written, illustrating the vast varieties of Shakespeare's art and power in this one field of improvement; another volume might be dedicated to the exposure of the lifeless and unnatural result from the opposite practice in the foreign stages of France and Italy. And we may truly say, that were Shakespeare distinguished from them by this single feature of nature and propriety, he would on that account alone have merited a great immortality.

Encyclopædia Britannica. 7th edition, 1838. Article on Shakespeare.

The following fine apostrophe to Shakespeare occurs at the end of De Quincey's essay "On the knocking at the gate in *Macbeth*":—O, mighty poet! Thy works are not as those of other men, simply and merely great works of art; but are also like the phenomena of nature, like the sun and the sea, the stars and the flowers,—like frost and snow, rain and dew, hailstorm and thunder, which are to be studied with entire submission of our own faculties, and in the perfect faith that in them there can be no too much or too little, nothing useless or inert,—but that, the further we press in our discoveries, the more we shall see proofs of design and self-supporting arrangement where the careless eye had seen nothing but accident.

JOHN STERLING, 1839
(1806-1844)

"Shakespeare."

> HOW little fades from earth when sink to rest
>
> The hours and cares that moved a great man's breast!
>
> Though nought of all we saw the grave may spare,
>
> His life pervades the world's impregnate air;
>
> Though Shakespeare's dust beneath our footsteps lies,
>
> His spirit breathes amid his native skies;
>
> With meaning won from him for ever glows
>
> Each air that England feels, and star it knows;
>
> His whispered words from many a mother's voice

Can make her sleeping child in dreams rejoice,

And gleams from spheres he first conjoined to earth

Are blent with rays of each new morning's birth.

Amid the sights and tales of common things,

Leaf, flower, and bird, and wars, and deaths of kings,

Of shore, and sea, and nature's daily round,

Of life that tills, and tombs that load the ground,

His visions mingle, swell, command, pace by,

And haunt with living presence heart and eye;

And tones from him by other bosoms caught

Awaken flush and stir of mounting thought,

And the long sigh, and deep impassioned thrill,

Rouse custom's trance, and spur the faltering will.

Above the goodly land more his than ours

He sits supreme enthroned in skyey towers,

And sees the heroic brood of his creation

Teach larger life to his ennobled nation.

O! shaping brain! O! flashing fancy's hues!

O! boundless heart kept fresh by pity's dews!

O! wit humane and blythe! O! sense sublime

For each dim oracle of mantled Time!

Transcendent Form of Man! in whom we read

Mankind's whole tale of impulse, thought, and deed;

Amid the expanse of years beholding thee,

We know how vast our world of life may be;

Wherein, perchance, with aims as pure as thine,

Small tasks and strengths may be no less divine.

Poems. 1839, p. 151.

HENRY HALLAM, 1839
(1777-1859)

OF William Shakespeare, whom, through the mouths of those whom he has inspired to body forth the modifications of his immense mind, we seem to know better than any human writer, it may be truly said that we scarcely know anything. We see him, so far as we do see him, not in himself, but in a reflex image from the objectivity in which he was manifested: he is Falstaff, and Mercutio, and Malvolio, and Jaques, and Portia, and Imogen, and Lear, and Othello; but to us he is scarcely a determined person, a substantial reality of past time, the man Shakespeare. The two greatest names in poetry are to us little more than names. If we are not yet come to question his unity, as we do that of "the blind old man of Scios' rocky isle," an improvement in critical acuteness doubtless reserved for a distant posterity, we as little feel the power of identifying the young man who came up from Stratford, was afterwards an indifferent player in a London theatre, and retired to his native place in middle life, with the author of Macbeth and Lear, as we can give a distinct historic personality to Homer. All that insatiable curiosity and unwearied diligence have hitherto detected about Shakespeare serves rather to disappoint and perplex us than to furnish the slightest illustration of his character.

Introduction to the Literature of Europe in the Fifteenth, Sixteenth, and Seventeenth Centuries. 1839, ii. 382-3.

—— JOHNSTONE, 1840

SOME men can only acquire knowledge by a careful process of painstaking investigation, while the minds of others descend at once, and with a swoop, as it were, upon the truth of which they are in search. Others, again, can not only do this, but having grasped the truth, they soar upward with it to the highest pinnacles of imaginative loftiness, or beyond these even, to the empyrean of thought, where the minds of ordinarily gifted men may not follow them. Of this last class was Shakespeare, the most wonderful of mere men that we know to have ever lived.

The Table Talker, or Brief Essays on Society and Literature. 1840, vol. i. p. 183.

THOMAS CARLYLE, 1840
(1795-1881)

"The Hero as Poet."

IT is in what I called Portrait-painting, delineating of men and things, especially of men, that Shakespeare is great. All the greatness of the man comes out decisively here. It is unexampled, I think, that calm creative perspicacity of Shakespeare. The thing he looks at reveals not this or that face of it, but its inmost heart and generic secret: it dissolves itself as in light before him, so that he discerns the perfect structure of it. Creative, we said; poetic creation, what is this too but *seeing* the thing sufficiently? The *word* that will describe the thing, follows of itself from such clear intense sight of the thing. And is not Shakespeare's *morality*, his valour, candour, tolerance, truthfulness; his whole victorious strength and greatness, which can triumph over such obstructions, visible there too? Great as the world! No *twisted*, poor convex-concave mirror, reflecting all objects with its own convexities and concavities; a perfectly *level* mirror;—that is to say withal, if we will understand it, a man justly related to all things and men, a good man. It is truly a lordly spectacle how this great soul takes in all kinds of men and objects, a Falstaff, an Othello, a Juliet, a Coriolanus; sets them all forth to us in their round completeness; loving, just, the equal brother of all. *Novum Organum*, and all the intellect you will find in Bacon, is of a quite secondary order; earthly, material, poor in comparison with this. Among modern men, one finds, in strictness, almost nothing of the same rank. Goethe alone, since the days of Shakespeare, reminds me of it. Of him too you say that he *saw* the object; you may say what he himself says of Shakespeare: "His characters are like watches with dial-plates of transparent crystal; they show you the hour like others, and the inward mechanism also is all visible."

On Heroes, Hero-Worship, and the Heroic in History. Ed. H. D. Traill. 1898, pp. 104-5.

In Carlyle's essay on "Corn Law Rhymes" (*Edinburgh Review*, July, 1832, p. 342) occurs the following:—Foolish Pedant, that sittest there compassionately descanting on the Learning of Shakespeare! Shakespeare had penetrated into innumerable things; far into Nature with her divine Splendours and infernal Terrors, her Ariel Melodies, and mystic mandragora Moans; far into man's workings with Nature, into man's Art and Artifice; Shakespeare knew (*Kenned*, which in those days still partially meant *Can-ned*) innumerable things; what men are, and what the world is, and how and what men aim at there, from the Dame Quickly of modern Eastcheap to the Cæsar of ancient Rome, over many countries, over many centuries: of all this he had the clearest understanding and constructive comprehension; all this was his Learning and Insight.

WILLIAM WORDSWORTH, 1841
(1770-1850)

"Shakespeare and Goethe."

HE (Goethe) does not seem to me to be a great poet in either of the classes of poets. At the head of the first class I would place Homer and Shakespeare, whose universal minds are able to reach every variety of thought and feeling without bringing their own individuality before the reader. They infuse, they breathe life into every object they approach, but you never find *themselves.* At the head of the second class, those whom you can trace individually in all they write, I would place Spenser and Milton. In all that Spenser writes you can trace the gentle affectionate spirit of the man; in all that Milton writes you find the exalted sustained being that he was. Now, in what Goethe writes, who aims to be of the first class, the *universal,* you find the man himself, the artificial man where he should not be found; so that I consider him a very artificial writer, aiming to be universal, and yet constantly exposing his individuality, which his character was not of a kind to dignify. He had not sufficiently clear moral perceptions to make him anything but an artificial writer.

Memoirs of William Wordsworth, by Christopher Wordsworth. 1851, vol. ii. pp. 437-8.

The value of this estimate of Goethe is somewhat discounted by a remark made at another time by Wordsworth: "I have tried to read Goethe. I never could succeed.... I am not intimately acquainted with them [his poems] generally." *Memoirs,* ii. p. 478.

THOMAS BABINGTON, LORD MACAULAY, 1843
(1800-1859)

HIGHEST among those who have exhibited human nature by means of dialogue stands Shakespeare. His variety is like the variety of nature, endless diversity, scarcely any monstrosity. The characters of which he has given us an impression, as vivid as that which we receive from the characters of our own associates, are to be reckoned by scores. Yet in all these scores hardly one character is to be found which deviates widely from the common standard, and which we should call very eccentric if we met it in real life. The silly notion that every man has one ruling passion, and that this clue, once known, unravels all the mysteries of his conduct, finds no countenance in the plays of Shakespeare. There man appears as he is, made up of a crowd of passions, which contend for the mastery over him, and govern him in turn. What is Hamlet's ruling passion? Or Othello's? Or

Harry the Fifth's? Or Wolsey's? Or Lear's? Or Shylock's? Or Benedick's? Or Macbeth's? Or that of Cassius? Or that of Falconbridge? But we might go on for ever. Take a single example, Shylock. Is he so eager for money as to be indifferent to revenge? Or so eager for revenge as to be indifferent to money? Or so bent on both together as to be indifferent to the honour of his nation and the law of Moses? All his propensities are mingled with each other, so that, in trying to apportion to each its proper part, we find the same difficulty which constantly meets us in real life. A superficial critic may say, that hatred is Shylock's ruling passion. But how many passions have amalgamated to form that hatred? It is partly the result of wounded pride: Antonio has called him dog. It is partly the result of covetousness: Antonio has hindered him of half a million; and, when Antonio is gone, there will be no limit to the gains of usury. It is partly the result of national and religious feeling: Antonio has spit on the Jewish gabardine; and the oath of revenge has been sworn by the Jewish Sabbath. We might go through all the characters which we have mentioned, and through fifty more in the same way; for it is the constant manner of Shakespeare to represent the human mind as lying, not under the absolute dominion of one despotic propensity, but under a mixed government, in which a hundred powers balance each other. Admirable as he is in all parts of his art, we most admire him for this, that while he has left us a greater number of striking portraits than all other dramatists put together, he has scarcely left us a single caricature.

Essay on "Diary and Letters of Madame D'Arblay," *Edinburgh Review*, Jan. 1843. Art. IX. vol. lxxvi. pp. 560-1.

RALPH WALDO EMERSON, 1844
(1803-1882)

SHAKESPEARE is the only biographer of Shakespeare; and even he can tell nothing except to the Shakespeare in us; that is, to our most apprehensive and sympathetic hour. He cannot step from off his tripod, and give us anecdotes of his inspirations. Read the antique documents extricated, analysed, and compared, by the assiduous Dyce and Collier; and now read one of those skiey sentences—aerolites,—which seem to have fallen out of heaven, and which, not your experience, but the man within the breast, has accepted as words of fate; and tell me if they match, if the former account in any manner for the latter: or, which gives the most historical insight into the man.

Hence, though our external history is so meagre, yet, with Shakespeare for biographer, instead of Aubrey and Rowe, we have really the information which is material, that which describes character and fortune, that which, if we were about to meet the man and deal with him, would most import us to know. We have his recorded convictions on those questions which knock for answer at every heart,—on life and death, on love, on wealth and poverty, on the prizes of life, and the ways whereby we come at them; on the characters of men, and the influences, occult and open, which affect their fortunes; and on those mysterious and demoniacal powers which defy our science, and which yet interweave their malice and their gift in our brightest hours. Whoever read the volume of the Sonnets, without finding that the poet had there revealed, under masks that are no masks to the intelligent, the lore of friendship and of love; the confusion of sentiments in the most susceptible, and, at the same time, the most intellectual of men? What trait of his private mind has he hidden in his dramas? One can discern, in his ample pictures of the gentleman and the king, that forms and humanities pleased him; his delight in troops of friends, in large hospitality, in cheerful giving. Let Timon, let Warwick, let Antonio the merchant, answer for his great heart. So far from Shakespeare's being the least known, he is the one person, in all modern history, known to us. What point of morals, of manners, of economy, of philosophy, of religion, of taste, of the conduct of life, has he not settled? What mystery has he not signified his knowledge of? What office, or function, or district of man's work, has he not remembered? What king has he not taught State, as Talma taught Napoleon? What maiden has not found him finer than her delicacy? What lover has he not outloved? What sage has he not outseen? What gentleman has he not instructed in the rudeness of his behaviour?

"Shakespeare; or, the Poet." *Representative Men.* 1844, p. 154.

FREDERICK WILLIAM ROBERTSON, 1850
(1816-1853)

WHAT I admire in Shakspeare, however, is that his loves are all human—no earthliness hiding itself from itself in sentimental transcendentalism—no loves of the angels, which are the least angelic things, I believe, that float in the clouds, though they do look down upon mortal feelings with contempt, just as the dark volumes of smoke which issue from the long chimney of a manufactory might brood very sublimely over the town which they blacken, and fancy themselves far more ethereal than those vapours which steam up from the earth by day and night. Yet these are pure water, and those are destined to condense in black soot. So are the transcendentalisms of affection. Shakspeare is healthy, true to Humanity in this: and for that reason I pardon him even his earthly coarseness. You always know that you are on an earth which has to be refined, instead of floating in the empyrean with wings of wax. Therein he is immeasurably greater than Shelley.

Shelleyism is very sublime, sublimer a good deal than God, for God's world is all wrong and Shelley is all right—much purer than Christ, for Shelley can criticise Christ's heart and life—nevertheless, Shelleyism is only atmospheric profligacy, to coin a Montgomeryism. I believe this to be one of Shakespeare's most wondrous qualities—the humanity of his nature and heart. There is a spirit of sunny endeavour about him, and an acquiescence in things as they are—not incompatible with a cheerful resolve to make them better.

Life and Letters of Frederick W. Robertson, M.A. Edited by Stopford A. Brooke, M.A. 1886, vol. i. p. 289, Letter LX.

LEIGH HUNT, 1851
(1784-1859)

"Associations with Shakespeare."

HOW naturally the idea of Shakespeare can be made to associate itself with anything which is worth mention! Take Christmas for instance: "Shakespeare and Christmas"; the two ideas fall as happily together as "wine and walnuts," or heart and soul. So you may put together "Shakespeare and May," or "Shakespeare and June," and twenty passages start into your memory about spring and violets. Or you may say "Shakespeare and Love," and you are in the midst of a bevy of bright damsels, as sweet as rosebuds; or "Shakespeare and Death," and all graves, and thoughts of graves, are before you; or "Shakespeare and Life," and you have the whole world of youth, and spirit, and Hotspur, and life itself; or you may say even, "Shakespeare and Hate," and he will say all that can be said for hate, as well as against it, till you shall take Shylock himself into your Christian arms, and tears shall make you of one faith.

Table Talk. 1851, p. 154.

JAMES ANTHONY FROUDE, 1852
(1818-1894)

WE wonder at the grandeur, the moral majesty of some of Shakespeare's characters, so far beyond what the noblest among ourselves can imitate, and at first thought we attribute it to the genius of the poet, who has outstripped nature in his creations. But we are misunderstanding the power and the meaning of poetry in attributing creativeness to it in any such sense. Shakespeare created, but only as the spirit of nature created around him, working in him as it worked abroad in those among whom he lived. The men whom he draws were such men as he saw and knew; the words they utter were such as he heard in the ordinary conversations in which he joined. At the Mermaid with Raleigh and with Sidney, and at a thousand unnamed English firesides, he found the living originals for his Prince Hals, his Orlandos, his Antonios, his Portias, his Isabellas. The closer personal acquaintance which we can form with the English of the age of Elizabeth, the more we are satisfied that Shakespeare's great poetry is no more than the rhythmic echo of the life which it depicts.

Short Studies on Great Subjects. First Series. "England's Forgotten Worthies." 1878, i. 445-6, reprinted from *Westminster Review*. 1852.

DAVID MASSON, 1853
(*b.* 1822)

SHAKESPEARE is as astonishing for the exuberance of his genius in abstract notions, and for the depth of his analytic and philosophic insight, as for the scope and minuteness of his poetic imagination. It is as if into a mind poetical in *form* there had been poured all the *matter* that existed in the mind of his contemporary Bacon. In Shakespeare's plays we have thought, history, exposition, philosophy, all within the round of the poet. The only difference between him and Bacon sometimes is that Bacon writes an essay and calls it his own, while Shakespeare writes a similar essay and puts it into the mouth of a Ulysses or a Polonius.

Wordsworth, Shelley, Keats, and Other Essays. 1874. Essay V. p. 242, reprinted from *North British Review*. 1853.

MATTHEW ARNOLD, 1853
(1822-1888)

"Shakespeare."

> OTHERS abide our question. Thou art free.
>
> We ask and ask—Thou smilest and art still,
>
> Out-topping knowledge. For the loftiest hill,
>
> Who to the stars uncrowns his majesty,
>
> Planting his steadfast footsteps in the sea,
>
> Making the heaven of heavens his dwelling-place,
>
> Spares but the cloudy border of his base
>
> To the foil'd searching of mortality;

And thou, who didst the stars and sunbeams know,

Self-school'd, self-scann'd, self-honour'd, self-secure,

Didst tread on earth unguessed at.—Better so!

All pains the immortal spirit must endure,

All weakness which impairs, all griefs which bow,

Find their sole speech in that victorious brow.

Poems. 1853.

WALTER SAVAGE LANDOR, 1853
(1775-1864)

"Shakespeare and Milton."

THE tongue of England, that which myriads

Have spoken and will speak, were paralysed

Hereafter, but two mighty men stand forth

Above the flight of ages, two alone;

One crying out,

All nations spoke thro' me.

The other:

True; and thro' this trumpet burst

God's word; the fall of Angels, and the doom

First of immortal, then of mortal, Man,

Glory! be glory! not to me, to God.

The Lost Fruit off an old Tree. No. LVII.

JOHN HENRY NEWMAN, 1858
(1801-1890)

A GREAT author, gentlemen, is not one who merely has a *copia verborum*, whether in prose or verse, and can, as it were, turn on at his will any number of splendid phrases and swelling sentences; but he is one who has something to say and knows how to say it. I do not claim for him, as such, any great depth of thought, or breadth of view, or philosophy, or sagacity, or knowledge of human nature, or experience of human life, though these additional gifts he may have, and the more he has of them the greater he is; but I ascribe to him, as his characteristic gift, in a large sense the faculty of Expression. He is master of the twofold Logos, the thought and the word, distinct, but inseparable from each other. He may, if so be, elaborate his compositions, or he may pour out his improvisations, but in either case he has but one aim, which he keeps steadily before him, and is conscientious and single-minded in fulfilling. That aim is to give forth what he has within him; and from his very earnestness it comes to pass that, whatever be the splendour of his diction or the harmony of his periods, he has with him the charm of an incommunicable simplicity. Whatever be his subject, high or low, he treats it suitably and for its own sake. If he is a poet, "nil molitur *inepte.*" If he is an orator, then too he speaks, not only "distincte" and "splendide," but also "apte." His page is the lucid mirror of his mind and life:

> "Quo fit, ut omnis
>
> Votivâ pateat veluti descripta labellâ
>
> Vita senis."

He writes passionately, because he feels keenly; forcibly, because he conceives vividly; he sees too clearly to be vague; he is too serious to be otiose; he can analyse his subject, and therefore he is rich; he embraces it as a whole and in its parts, and therefore he is consistent; he has a firm hold of it, and therefore he is luminous; when his imagination wells up, it overflows its ornament; when his heart is touched, it thrills along his verse. He always has the right word for the right idea, and never a word too much. If he is brief, it is because few words suffice; when he is lavish of them, still each word has its mark, and aids, not embarrasses, the vigorous march of his elocution. He expresses what all feel, but all cannot say; and his sayings pass into proverbs among his people, and his phrases become household words and idioms of their daily speech, which is tessellated with the rich fragments of his language, as we see in foreign lands the marbles of Roman grandeur worked into the walls and pavements of modern palaces.

Such pre-eminently is Shakespeare among ourselves; such pre-eminently is Virgil among the Latins; such in their degree are all those writers who in every nation go by the name of Classics.

"The Idea of a University defined and illustrated." *Literature*, ix. 1873, pp. 291-3.

JAMES RUSSELL LOWELL, *c.* 1858
(1819-1891)

ONLY Shakespeare was endowed with that healthy equilibrium of nature whose point of rest was midway between the imagination and the understanding,—that perfectly unruffled brain which reflected all objects with almost inhuman impartiality,—that outlook whose range was ecliptical, dominating all zones of human thought and action,—that power of verisimilar conception which could take away Richard III. from History, and Ulysses from Homer,—and that creative faculty whose equal touch is alike vivifying in Shallow and in Lear. He alone never seeks in abnormal and monstrous characters to evade the risks and responsibilities of absolute truthfulness, nor to stimulate a jaded imagination by Caligulan horrors of plot. He is never, like many of his fellow-dramatists, confronted with unnatural Frankensteins of his own making, whom he must get off his hands as best he may. Given a human foible, he can incarnate it in the nothingness of Slender, or make it loom gigantic through the tragic twilight of Hamlet. We are tired of the vagueness which classes all the Elizabethan playwrights together as "great dramatists,"—as if Shakespeare did not differ from them in kind as well as in degree. Fine poets some of them were; but though imagination and the power of poetic expression are, singly, not uncommon gifts, and even in combination not without secular examples, yet it is the rarest of earthly phenomena to find them joined with those faculties of perception, arrangement, and plastic instinct in the loving union which alone makes a great dramatic poet possible. We suspect that Shakespeare will long continue the only specimen of the genus. His contemporaries, in their comedies, either force what they call "a humour" till it becomes fantastical, or hunt for jokes, like rat-catchers, in the sewers of human nature and of language. In their tragedies they become heavy without grandeur, like Jonson, or mistake the stilts for the cothurnus, as Chapman and Webster too often do. Every new edition of an Elizabethan dramatist is but the putting of another witness into the box to prove the inaccessibility of Shakespeare's standpoint as poet and artist.

Library of Old Authors. 1858-64.

For an interesting note on Shakespeare's "artistic discretion" and the "impersonality" of his writings, see "Shakespeare once more" (*Among My Books.* 1870, pp. 226-7).

NATHANIEL HAWTHORNE, 1863
(1804-1864)

SHAKESPEARE has surface beneath surface, to an immeasurable depth, adapted to the plummet-line of every reader; his works present many phases of truth, each with scope large enough to fill a contemplative mind. Whatever you seek in him you will surely discover, provided you seek truth. There is no exhausting the various interpretation of his symbols; and a thousand years hence, a world of new readers will possess a whole library of new books, as we ourselves do, in these volumes old already.

Our Old Home. 1863, i. 171.

In *Our Old Home* (i. 158-60) Hawthorne records his impressions on visiting Shakespeare's house.

BISHOP CHARLES WORDSWORTH, 1864
(1806-1892)

TAKE the entire range of English literature; put together our best authors, who have written upon subjects not professedly religious or theological, and we shall not find, I believe, in them *all united,* so much evidence of the Bible having been read and used, as we have found in Shakespeare *alone.* This is a phenomenon which admits of being looked at from several points of view; but I shall be content to regard it solely in connection with the undoubted fact, that of all our authors, Shakespeare is also, by general confession, the greatest and the best. According to the testimony of Charles Lamb, a most competent judge in regard to all the literary elements of the question, our poet, "in his divine mind and manners, surpassed not only the great men his contemporaries, but all mankind." And, looking at this superiority from my own point of view, I cannot but remark that, while most of the great laymen of that great Elizabethan age—Lord Bacon, Sir Walter Raleigh, the poet Spenser, Sir Philip Sidney, Lord Burleigh, Ben Jonson—have paid homage to Christianity, if not always in their practice, yet in the conviction of their understanding, none of them has done this so fully or so effectively as Shakespeare.

"On Shakespeare's Knowledge and Use of the Bible." 1864, pp. 291-2.

OLIVER WENDELL HOLMES, 1864
(1809-1894)

> O LAND of Shakespeare! ours with all thy past,
>
> Till these last years that make the sea so wide,

Think not the jar of battle's trumpet-blast
Has dulled our aching sense to joyous pride
In every noble word thy sons bequeathed
The air our fathers breathed!

War-wasted, haggard, panting from the strife,
We turn to other days and far-off lands,
Live o'er in dreams the Poet's faded life,
Come with fresh lilies in our fevered hands
To wreathe his bust, and scatter purple flowers,—
Not his the need, but ours!

We call those poets who are first to mark
Through earth's dull mist the coming of the dawn,—
Who see in twilight's gloom the first pale spark,
While others only note that day is gone;
For him the Lord of light the curtain rent
That veils the firmament . . .

With no vain praise we mock the stone-carved name
Stamped once on dust that moved with pulsed breath,
As thinking to enlarge that amplest fame
Whose undimmed glories gild the night of death:
We praise not star or sun; in these we see
Thee, Father, only Thee!

Thy gifts are beauty, wisdom, power, and love:
We read, we reverence on this human soul,—
Earth's clearest mirror of the light above,—
Plain as the record on Thy prophet's scroll,
When o'er his page the effluent splendours poured,
Thine own, "Thus saith the Lord!"

This player was a prophet from on high,

Thine own elected. Statesman, poet, sage,

For him Thy sovereign pleasure passed them by;

Sidney's fair youth, and Raleigh's ripened age,

Spenser's chaste soul, and his imperial mind

Who taught and shamed mankind.

"Shakespeare Tercentennial Celebration, 23 April 1864." *Songs of Many Seasons*. 1875.

CARDINAL WISEMAN, 1865
(1802-1865)

WE may compare the mind of Shakespeare to a diamond, pellucid, bright, and untinted, cut into countless polished facets, which, in constant movement, at every smallest change of direction or of angle, caught a new reflection, so that not one of its brilliant mirrors could be for a moment idle, but by a power beyond its control was ever busy with the reflection of innumerable images, either distinct or running into one another, or repeated each so clearly as to allow him, when he chose, to fix it in his memory.

William Shakespeare. 1865, p. 50.

ARCHBISHOP RICHARD CHENEVIX TRENCH, 1865
(1807-1886)

A COUNSELLOR well fitted to advise

In daily life, and at whose lips no less

Men may inquire or nations, when distress

Of sudden doubtful danger may arise,

Who, though his head be hidden in the skies,

Plants his firm foot upon our common earth,

Dealing with thoughts which everywhere have birth,—

This is the poet, true of heart and wise:

No dweller in a baseless world of dream,

Which is not earth nor heaven: his words have passed

Into man's common thought and week-day phrase;

This is the poet and his verse will last.

Such was our Shakespeare once, and such doth seem

One who redeems our later gloomier days.

Poems collected and arranged anew. 1865, p. 83.

FRANCIS TURNER PALGRAVE, 1865
(1824-1897)

ONLY three or four generations of fairly long-lived men lie between us and Shakespeare; literature in his own time had reached a high development; his grandeur and sweetness were freely recognised; within seventy years of his death his biography was attempted; yet we know little more of Shakespeare himself than we do of Homer. Like several of the greatest men,—Lucretius, Virgil, Tacitus, Dante,—a mystery never to be dispelled hangs over his life. He has entered into the cloud. With a natural and an honourable diligence, other men have given their lives to the investigation of his, and many external circumstances, mostly of a minor order, have been thus collected: yet of "the man Shakespeare," in Mr. Hallam's words, we know nothing. Something which seems more than human in immensity of range and calmness of insight moves before us in the Plays; but, from the nature of dramatic writing, the author's personality is inevitably veiled; no letter, no saying of his, or description by an intimate friend, has been preserved: and even when we turn to the *Sonnets*, though each is an autobiographical confession, we find ourselves equally foiled. These revelations of the poet's innermost nature appear to teach us less of the man than the tone of mind which we trace, or seem to trace, in *Measure for Measure*, *Hamlet*, and the *Tempest*: the strange imagery of passion which passes over the magic mirror has no tangible existence before or behind it:—the great artist, like Nature herself, is still latent in his works; diffused through his own creation.

......

Yet there is, after all, nothing more remarkable or fascinating in English poetry than these personal revelations of the mind of our greatest poet. We read them again and again, and find each time some new proof of his almost superhuman insight into human nature; of his unrivalled mastery over all the tones of love.

Songs and Sonnets of William Shakespeare. Edited by Francis Turner Palgrave. 1865, pp. 238-9 and 243.

FRANCES ANNE KEMBLE, 1866
(1809-1893)

"To Shakespeare."

> SHELTER and succour such as common men
>
> Afford the weaker partners of their fate,
>
> Have I derived from thee—from thee, most great
>
> And powerful genius! whose sublime control
>
> Still from thy grave governs each human soul,
>
> That reads the wondrous record of thy pen.
>
> From sordid sorrows thou hast set me free,
>
> And turned from want's grim ways my tottering feet,
>
> And to sad empty hours, given royally,
>
> A labour, than all leisure far more sweet.
>
> The daily bread, for which we humbly pray,
>
> Thou gavest me as if I were a child,
>
> And still with converse noble, wise, and mild,
>
> Charmed with despair my sinking soul away;
>
> Shall I not bless the need, to which was given
>
> Of all the angels in the host of heaven,
>
> Thee, for my guardian, spirit strong and bland!
>
> Lord of the speech of my dear native land!

Poems. 1866, p. 61.

JOHN RUSKIN, 1868
(1819-1900)

IT does not matter how little, or how much, any of us have read, either of Homer, or Shakespeare: everything round us, in substance, or in thought, has been moulded by them. All Greek gentlemen were educated under Homer. All Roman gentlemen by Greek literature. All Italian, and French, and English gentlemen, by Roman literature, and by its principles. Of the scope of Shakespeare, I will say only, that the intellectual measure of every man since born, in the domains of creative thought, may be assigned to him, according to the degree in which he has been taught by Shakespeare.

The Mystery of Life and its Arts. Afternoon Lectures on Literature and Art, delivered at Royal College of Science, St. Stephen's Green, Dublin, 1867 and 1868. 1869, p. 109.

DANTE GABRIEL ROSSETTI, 1871
(1828-1882)

"On the Site of a Mulberry-Tree."

Planted by William Shakespeare; felled by the Rev. F. Gastrell.

> THIS tree, here fall'n, no common birth or death
>
> Shared with its kind. The world's enfranchised son,
>
> Who found the trees of Life and Knowledge one,
>
> Here set it, frailer than his laurel-wreath.
>
> Shall not the wretch whose hand it fell beneath
>
> Rank also singly—the supreme unhung?
>
> Lo! Sheppard, Turpin, pleading with black tongue,
>
> This viler thief's unsuffocated breath!
>
> We'll search thy glossary, Shakespeare! whence almost,
>
> And whence alone, some name shall be reveal'd
>
> For this deaf drudge, to whom no length of years
>
> Sufficed to catch the music of the spheres;
>
> Whose soul is carrion now,—too mean to yield
>
> Some Starveling's ninth allotment of a ghost.

Academy, 15 Feb. 1871.[185:1] *Collected Works.* Ed. W. M. Rossetti. 1886, vol. i. p. 285.

BAYARD TAYLOR, 1872
(1825-1878)

HERE, in his right, he stands!

No breadth of earth-dividing seas can bar

The breeze of morning, or the morning star,

From visiting our lands:

His wit the breeze, his wisdom as the star,

Shone where our earliest life was set, and blew

To freshen hope and plan

In brains American,—

To urge, resist, encourage, and subdue!

He came, a household ghost we could not ban:

He sat, on winter nights, by cabin fires;

His summer fairies linked their hands

Along our yellow sands;

He preached within the shadow of our spires;

And when the certain Fate drew nigh, to cleave

The birth-cord, and a separate being leave,

He, in our ranks of patient-hearted men,

Wrought with the boundless forces of his fame,

Victorious, and became

The Master of our thought, the land's first Citizen!

If, here, his image seem

Of softer scenes and grayer skies to dream,

Thatched cot and rustic tavern, ivied hall,

The cuckoo's April call

And cowslip-meads beside the Avon stream,

He shall not fail that other home to find
We could not leave behind!
The forms of Passion, which his fancy drew,
In us their ancient likenesses beget:
So, from our lives for ever born anew,
He stands amid his own creations yet!
Here comes lean Cassius, of conventions tired;
Here, in his coach, luxurious Antony
Beside his Egypt, still of men admired;
And Brutus plans some purer liberty!
A thousand Shylocks, Jew and Christian, pass;
A hundred Hamlets, by their times betrayed;
And sweet Anne Page comes tripping o'er the grass,
And awkward Falstaff pants beneath the shade.
Here toss upon the wanton summer wind
The locks of Rosalind;
Here some gay glove the damned spot conceals
Which Lady Macbeth feels:
His ease here smiling smooth Iago takes,
And outcast Lear gives passage to his woe,
And here some foiled Reformer sadly breaks
His wand of Prospero!
In liveried splendour, side by side,
Nick Bottom and Titania ride,
And Portia, flushed with cheers of men,
Disdains dear faithful Imogen;
And Puck beside the form of Morse,
Stops on his forty-minute course;
And Ariel from his swinging bough

A blossom casts on Bryant's brow,

Until, as summoned from his brooding brain,

He sees his children all again,

In us, as on our lips, each fresh, immortal strain!

Poetical Works. Stanzas II.-III. 1880, p. 224.

WILLIAM MINTO, 1874
(1845-1893)

IT is a favourite way with some eulogists of Shakespeare to deny him all individuality whatsoever. He was not one man, they say, but an epitome of all men. His mind, says Hazlitt, "had no one peculiar bias or exclusive excellence more than another. He was just like any other man, but that he was like all other men. He was the least of an egotist that it was possible to be. He was nothing in himself; but he was all that others were or that they could become." Against such a degradation of Shakespeare's character, or of any man's character, it is our duty to protest. On trying to make Shakespeare more than human, the reckless panegyrist makes him considerably less than human: instead of the man whose prudence made him rich, whose affectionate nature made him loved almost to idolatry, and whose genius has been the wonder of the world, we are presented with plasticity in the abstract, an object not more interesting than a quarry of potter's clay.

"William Shakespeare, his Life and Character." *Characteristics of English Poets.* 1874, p. 350.

See the passage from Hazlitt's *Lectures on the English Poets*, p. <u>135</u>.

EDWARD DOWDEN, 1875
(*b.* 1843)

THERE are certain problems which Shakespeare at once pronounces insoluble. He does not, like Milton, propose to give any account of the origin of evil. He does not, like Dante, pursue the soul of man through circles of unending torture, or spheres made radiant by the eternal presence of God. Satan, in Shakespeare's poems, does not come voyaging on gigantic vans across Chaos to find the earth. No great deliverer of mankind descends from the heavens. Here, upon the earth, evil *is*—such was Shakespeare's declaration in the most emphatic accent. Iago actually exists.

There is also in the earth a sacred passion of deliverance, a pure redeeming ardour. Cordelia exists. This Shakespeare can tell for certain. But how Iago can be, and why Cordelia lies strangled across the breast of Lear—are these questions which you go on to ask? Something has been already said of the severity of Shakespeare. It is a portion of his severity to decline all answers to such questions as these. Is ignorance painful? Well, then, it is painful. Little solutions of your large difficulties can readily be obtained from priest or *philosopher*. Shakespeare prefers to let you remain in the solemn presence of a mystery. He does not invite you into his little church or his little library brilliantly illuminated by philosophical or theological rushlights. You remain in the darkness. But you remain in the vital air. And the great night is overhead.

Shakspere: A Critical Study of his Mind and Art. 1875, p. 226.

GEORGE MEREDITH, 1877
(*b.* 1828)

SHAKESPEARE is a well-spring of characters which are saturated with the comic spirit; with more of what we will call blood-life than is to be found anywhere out of Shakespeare; and they are of this world, but they are of the world enlarged to our embrace by imagination, and by great poetic imagination. They are, as it were—I put it to suit my present comparison— creatures of the woods and wilds, not in walled towns, not grouped and toned to pursue a comic exhibition of the narrower world of society. Jaques, Falstaff and his regiment, the varied troop of clowns, Malvolio, Sir Hugh Evans and Fluellen—marvellous Welshmen!—Benedict and Beatrice, Dogberry, and the rest, are subjects of a special study in the poetically comic.

On the Idea of Comedy and of the Uses of the Comic Spirit. A lecture delivered at the London Institution, 1 Feb. 1877. Published 1897.

FREDERICK JAMES FURNIVALL, 1877
(*b.* 1825)

ALTOGETHER "a manly man" (as Chaucer says) this Shakespeare, strong, tender, humourful, sensitive, impressionable, the truest friend, the foe of none but narrow minds and base. And as we track his work from the lightness and fun of its rise, through the fairy fancy, the youthful passion, the rich imaginings, the ardent patriotism, the brilliant sunshine, of his first and second times, through the tender affection of his Sonnets, the whirlwind of passions in his Tragedies, and then to the lovely sunset of his latest plays, what can we do but bless his name, and be thankful that he came to be a delight, a lift and strength, to us and our children's children to all time—a bond that shall last for ever between all English-speaking, English-reading men, the members of that great Teutonic brotherhood which shall yet long lead the world in the fight for freedom and for truth!

Introduction to *The Leopold Shakspere*.1877, p. cxvi.

WALTER HORATIO PATER, 1878
(1839-1894)

AS happens with every true dramatist, Shakespeare is for the most part hidden behind the persons of his creation. Yet there are certain of his characters in which we feel that there is something of self-portraiture. And it is not so much in his grander, more subtle and ingenious creations that we feel this—in "Hamlet" and "King Lear"—as in those slighter and more spontaneously developed figures, who, while far from playing principal parts, are yet distinguished by a peculiar happiness and delicate ease in the drawing of them; figures which possess, above all, that winning attractiveness which there is no man but would willingly exercise, and which resemble those works of art which, though not meant to be very great or imposing, are yet wrought of the choicest material. Mercutio, in "Romeo and Juliet," belongs to this group of Shakespeare's characters— versatile, mercurial people, such as make good actors, and in whom the

"Nimble spirits of the arteries,"

the finer but still merely animal elements of great wit, predominate. A careful delineation of minor yet expressive traits seems to mark them out as the characters of his predilection; and it is hard not to identify him with these more than with others. Biron, in "Love's Labour's Lost," is perhaps the most striking member of this group. In this character, which is never quite in touch, never quite on a perfect level of understanding, with the other persons of the play, we see, perhaps, a reflex of Shakespeare himself, when he has just become able to stand aside from and estimate the first period of his poetry.

"Love's Labour's Lost." *Appreciations with an Essay on Style*. 1889, pp. 174-5.

See also "Shakspere's English Kings," *ib.*, pp. 201-2.

MATTHEW ARNOLD, 1879
(1822-1888)

LET me have the pleasure of quoting a sentence about Shakespeare, which I met with by accident not long ago in the *Correspondant*, a French review which not a dozen English people, I suppose, look at. The writer is praising Shakespeare's prose. "With Shakespeare," he says, "prose comes in whenever the subject, being more familiar, is unsuited to the majestic English iambic." And he goes on: "Shakespeare is the king of poetic rhythm and style, as well as the king of the realm of thought; along with his dazzling prose, Shakespeare has succeeded in giving us the most varied, the most harmonious verse which has ever sounded upon the human ear since the verse of the Greeks." M. Henry Cochin, the writer of this sentence, deserves our gratitude for it; it would not be easy to praise Shakespeare, in a single sentence, more justly. And when a foreigner and a Frenchman writes thus of Shakespeare, and when Goethe says of Milton, in whom there was so much to repel Goethe rather than to attract him, that "nothing has ever been done so entirely in the sense of the Greeks as *Samson Agonistes*," and that "Milton is in very truth a poet whom we must treat with all reverence," then we understand what constitutes a European recognition of poets and poetry as contradistinguished from a merely national recognition, and that in favour both of Milton and of Shakespeare the judgment of the high court of appeal has finally gone.

Essays in Criticism. Second Series: Wordsworth. 1888, pp. 129-31. Reprinted from Preface to *The Poems of Wordsworth*, chosen and edited by Matthew Arnold. 1879.

For a comment on Shakespeare's double faculty of interpreting the physiognomy and movement of the outward world, and the ideas and laws of man's moral and spiritual nature, see *Essays in Criticism*, 1865, p. 108.

ANONYMOUS ?c. 1880

SO much has been written, so much spoken about Shakespeare, that it would seem a needless, almost a presumptuous superfluity to say more, and yet from another point of view, the man is as strange to us to-day as though we had never heard his name. Johnson and Pope, Warburton, Steevens, Malone and Theobald, Chalmers, Dyce, and a host of foreign exegetes, have edited and annotated, emendated and obelised; but the figure of Shakespeare is clothed in mist, and whilst we laugh and wonder at the vanity and versatility of a Cicero, and stroll lovingly with a Horace about his Sabine farm, dead both of them two millennia, we still grope about in the dark for the meaning, the character, and the inner life of our wondrous poet. Like the ghost in Hamlet, he arose, and, having uttered his pregnant message, disappeared, unregarded at the time but by a few, and still unrealised by the many.

....

There is a grandeur about the poets of the world, and a reward for those that study them aright. Amid the hurricane of battle and the crash of empires, the calm pulse of life and the glories of the drama remain the same. Men are inclined to gaze upon the outward symbols of existence as though they were primary causes, when they are only the emblems of a deeper power. We have had our Constitution-builders, but where are they? Our Tamerlanes and our Attilas, but whither are they departed? The intellect that revolves a kingdom pales before a heart that speaks to the soul of man. All nations turn their faces toward a Hamlet, a Lear, or a Catherine of Aragon. The influence of these through the genius of the poet will spread and yield abundant fruit, when the havoc of a Cannæ or an Austerlitz is but dimly discernible in the skeleton of history.

The study of our finer literature is therefore the study of the soul; and the progress made will be upward and inward, and the result a purifying of the ideals and a chastening of the chords of man. Shakespeare gives us all this, he is ennobling as well as instructive; without paying homage in a measure to his memory by the maintenance of a certain form of excellence, no poet since his time has succeeded in being appreciated as great. For they all bear his mark, and although much below him, all dramatic writers since his day are modelled upon his plan.

Manuscript Note inserted before fly-leaf of copy of the 1602 quarto of *Merry Wives of Windsor*, now in Rowfant Library. Printed in *A Catalogue of the Printed Books, etc., collected since 1886 by the late Frederick Locker Lampson.* 1900, pp. 28-30.

ALGERNON CHARLES SWINBURNE, 1880
(*b.* 1837)

IN his first stage Shakespeare had dropped his plummet no deeper into the sea of the spirit of man than Marlowe had sounded before him; and in the channel of simple emotion no poet could cast surer line with steadier hand than he. Further down in the dark and fiery depths of human pain and mortal passion no soul could search than his who first rendered into speech the aspirations and the agonies of a ruined and revolted spirit. And until Shakespeare found in himself the strength of eyesight to read, and the cunning of handiwork to render those wider diversities of emotion and those further complexities of character which lay outside the range of Marlowe, he certainly cannot be said to have outrun the winged feet, outstripped the fiery flight of his forerunner. In the heaven of our tragic song, the first-born star on the forehead of its herald god was not outshone till the full midsummer meridian of that greater godhead before whom he was sent to prepare a pathway for the sun. Through all the forenoon of our triumphant day, till the utter consummation and ultimate ascension of dramatic poetry incarnate and transfigured in the master-singer of the world, the quality of his tragedy was as that of Marlowe's, broad, single, and intense; large of hand, voluble of tongue, direct of purpose. With the dawn of its latter epoch a new power comes upon it, to find clothing and expression in new forms of speech and after a new style. The language has put off its foreign decorations of lyric and elegiac ornament; it has found already its infinite gain in the loss of those sweet superfluous graces which encumbered the march and enchained the utterance of its childhood. The figures which it invests are now no more types of a single passion, the incarnations of a single thought. They now demand a scrutiny which tests the power of a mind and tries the value of a judgment; they appeal to something more than the instant apprehension which sufficed to respond to the immediate claim of those that went before them. Romeo and Juliet were simply lovers, and their names bring back to us no further thought than of their love and the lovely sorrow of its end; Antony and Cleopatra shall be before all things lovers, but the thought of their love and its triumphant tragedy shall recall other things beyond number—all the forces and all the fortunes of mankind, all the chance and all the consequence that waited on their imperial passion, all the infinite variety of qualities and powers wrought together and welded into the frame and composition of that love which shook from end to end all nations and kingdoms of the earth.

A Study of Shakespeare. 1880, pp. 77-9.

ALGERNON CHARLES SWINBURNE, 1882
(*b.* 1837)

"William Shakespeare."

> NOT if men's tongues and angels' all in one
>
> Spake, might the word be said that might speak thee.
>
> Streams, winds, woods, flowers, fields, mountains, yea the sea,
>
> What power is in them all to praise the sun?

His praise is this,—he can be praised of none.

Man, woman, child, praise God for him; but he

Exults not to be worshipped, but to be.

He is; and, being, beholds his work well done.

All joy, all glory, all sorrow, all strength, all mirth,

Are his: without him, day were night on earth.

Time knows not his from time's own period.

All lutes, all harps, all viols, all flutes, all lyres,

Fall dumb before him ere one string suspires.

All stars are angels; but the sun is God.

Tristram of Lyonesse and other Poems. 1882, p. 280.

See also Mr. Swinburne's *An Autumn Vision, October 31, 1889.*

GEORGE MEREDITH, 1883
(*b.* 1828)

"The Spirit of Shakespeare."

THY greatest knew thee, Mother Earth; unsoured

He knew thy sons. He probed from hell to hell

Of human passions, but of love deflowered

His wisdom was not, for he knew thee well.

Thence came the honeyed corner of his lips,

The conquering smile wherein his spirit sails

Calm as the God who the white sea-wave whips,

Yet full of speech and intershifting tales,

Close mirrors of us: thence had he the laugh

We feel is thine: broad as ten thousand beeves

At pasture! thence thy songs, that winnow chaff

From grain, bid sick Philosophy's last leaves

Whirl, if they have no recompense—they enforced

To fatten Earth when from her soul divorced.

How smiles he at a generation ranked

In gloomy noddings over life! They pass.

Not he to feed upon a breast unthanked,

Or eye a beauteous face in a cracked glass.

But he can spy that little twist of brain

Which moved some mighty leader of the blind,

Unwitting 'twas the goad of personal pain,

To view in curst eclipse our Mother's mind,

And show us of some rigid harridan

The wretched bondman till the end of time.

O lived the Master now to paint us Man,

That little twist of brain would ring a chime

Of whence it came and what it caused, to start

Thunders of laughter, clearing air and heart.

Poems and Lyrics of the Joy of Earth. 1883, pp. 161-2.

ROBERT BROWNING, 1884
(1812-1889)

"The Names."

SHAKESPEARE!—to such name's sounding, what succeeds

Fitly as a silence? Falter forth the spell,—

Act follows word, the speaker knows full well,

Nor tampers with its magic more than needs.

Two names there are: That which the Hebrew reads

With his soul only: if from lips it fell,

Echo, back thundered by earth, heaven and hell,

Would own, "Thou didst create us!" Nought impedes

We voice the other name, man's most of might,

Awesomely, lovingly: let awe and love

Mutely await their working, leave to sight

All of the issue as below—above—

Shakespeare's creation rises: one remove

Though dread—this finite from that infinite.

Complete Poetic and Dramatic Works of Robert Browning. Cambridge edition, U.S.A. 1895.

Browning wrote this sonnet as a contribution to the *Shakespearean Show-Book* issued at the "Shakespearean Show" held in the Albert Hall, London, 29-31 May 1884, in aid of the Hospital for Women in Fulham Road. The sonnet is dated 12 March 1884.

WILLIAM WETMORE STORY, 1886
(*b.* 1819)

"The Mighty Makers."

WHOSE are those forms august that, in the press

And busy blames and praises of to-day,

Stand so serene above life's fierce affray

With ever youthful strength and loveliness?

Those are the mighty makers, whom no stress

Of time can shame, nor fashion sweep away,

Whom Art begot on Nature in the play

Of healthy passion, scorning base excess.

Rising perchance in mists, and half obscure

When up the horizon of their age they came,

Brighter with years they shine in steadier light,

Great constellations that will aye endure,

Though myriad meteors of ephemeral fame

Across them flash, to vanish into night.

Such was our Chaucer in the early prime

Of English verse, who held to Nature's hand

And walked serenely through its morning land,

Gladsome and hale, brushing its dewy rime.

And such was Shakespeare, whose strong soul could climb

Steeps of sheer terror, sound the ocean grand

Of passions deep, or over Fancy's strand

Trip with his fairies, keeping step and time.

His too the power to laugh out full and clear,

With unembittered joyance, and to move

Along the silent, shadowy paths of love

As tenderly as Dante, whose austere

Stern spirit through the worlds below, above,

Unsmiling strode, to tell their tidings here.

Poems. 1886, vol. ii. pp. 273-4.

THOMAS SPENCER BAYNES, 1886
(1823-1887)

SHAKESPEARE'S work alone can be said to possess the organic strength and infinite variety, the throbbing fulness, vital complexity, and breathing truth of Nature herself. In points of artistic resource and technical ability—such as copious and expressive diction, freshness and pregnancy of verbal combination, richly modulated verse, and structural skill in the handling of incident and action—Shakespeare's supremacy is indeed sufficiently assured. But, after all, it is of course in the spirit and substance of his work, his power of piercing to the hidden centres of character, of touching the deepest springs of impulse and passion, out of which are the issues of life, and of evolving those issues dramatically with a flawless strength, subtlety, and truth, which raises him so immensely above and beyond not only the best of the playwrights who went before him, but the whole line of illustrious dramatists that came after him. It is Shakespeare's unique distinction that he has an absolute command over all the complexities of thought and feeling that prompt to action and bring out the dividing lines of character. He sweeps with the hand of a master the whole gamut of human experience, from the lowest note to the very top of its compass, from the sportive childish treble of Mamilius, and the pleading boyish tones of Prince Arthur, up to the spectre-haunted terrors of Macbeth, the tropical passion of Othello, the agonised sense and tortured spirit of Hamlet, the sustained elemental grandeur, the Titanic force, the utterly tragical pathos of Lear.

Encyclopædia Britannica. 9th edition. Art. "Shakespeare." Vol. xxi. 1886, p. 763.

GERALD MASSEY, 1888
(*b.* 1828)

> OUR Prince of Peace in glory hath gone,
>
> With no Spear shaken, no Sword drawn,
>
> No Cannon fired, no flag unfurled,
>
> To make his conquest of the World.
>
> For him no Martyr-fires have blazed,
>
> No limbs been racked, no scaffolds raised;
>
> For him no life was ever shed,
>
> To make the Victor's pathway red.
>
> And for all time he wears the Crown
>
> Of lasting, limitless renown:
>
> He reigns, whatever Monarchs fall;
>
> His Throne is in the heart of all.

The Secret Drama of Shakespeare's Sonnets. 1888.

WALT WHITMAN, 1890
(1819-1892)

THE inward and outward characteristics of Shakespeare are his vast and rich variety of persons and themes, with his wondrous delineation of each and all—not only limitless funds of verbal and pictorial resource, but great excess, superfœtation—mannerism, like a fine aristocratic perfume, holding a touch of musk (Euphues, his mark)—with boundless sumptuousness and adornment, real velvet and gems, not shoddy nor paste—but a good deal of bombast and fustian—(certainly some terrific mouthing in Shakespeare!).

Superb and inimitable as all is, it is mostly an objective and physiological kind of power and beauty the soul finds in Shakespeare—a style supremely grand of the sort, but in my opinion stopping short of the grandest sort, at any rate for fulfilling and satisfying modern and scientific and democratic American purposes. Think, not of growths as forests primeval, or Yellowstone geysers, or Colorado ravines, but of costly marble palaces, and palace rooms, and the noblest fixings and furniture, and noble owners and occupants to correspond—think of carefully built gardens from the beautiful but sophisticated gardening art at its best, with walks and bowers and artificial lakes, and appropriate statue groups, and the finest cultivated roses and lilies and japonicas in plenty—and you have the tally of Shakespeare. The low characters, mechanics, even the loyal henchmen—all in themselves nothing—serve as capital foils to the aristocracy. The comedies (exquisite as they certainly are), bringing in admirably portrayed common characters, have the unmistakable hue of plays, portraits, made for the divertisement only of the élite of the castle, and from its point of view. The comedies are altogether non-acceptable to America and Democracy.

But to the deepest soul, it seems a shame to pick and choose from the riches Shakespeare has left us—to criticise his infinitely royal, multiform quality—to gauge, with optic glasses, the dazzle of his sun-like beams.

From *Poet-Lore*, July 1890. *Complete Prose Works*. Boston, Mass., 1898, p. 394.

Walt Whitman, when he says that "the comedies are altogether non-acceptable to America and Democracy," states rather what he considers ought to be, than what actually is. In his essay, "Poetry To-day in America," he says of Shakespeare, "In portraying mediæval European lords and barons, the arrogant poet, so dear to the inmost human heart (pride! pride! dearest, perhaps, of all—touching us, too, of the States closest of all—closer than love), he stands alone, and I do not wonder he so witches the world."—*Prose Works*, Boston, 1898, p. 283.

RICHARD WATSON GILDER, 1891
(*b.* 1844)

"The Twenty-Third of April."

> A LITTLE English earth and breathèd air
>
> Made Shakespeare the divine; so is his verse

The broidered soil of every blossom fair;

So doth his song all sweet bird-songs rehearse.

But tell me, then, what wondrous stuff did fashion

That part of him which took those wilding flights

Among imagined worlds; whence the white passion

That burned three centuries through the days and nights!

Not heaven's four winds could make, nor round the earth,

The soul wherefrom the soul of Hamlet flamed;

Nor anything of merely mortal birth

Could lighten as when Shakespeare's name is named.

How was his body bred we know full well,

But that high soul's engendering who may tell!

"Five Books of Song." IV. *The Two Worlds*. 1894, p. 154.

MATHILDE BLIND, *c.* 1894
(1841-1896)

"Shakespeare."

YEARNING to know herself for all she was,

Her passionate clash of warring good and ill,

Her new life ever ground in Death's old mill,

With every delicate detail and *en masse*,—

Blind Nature strove. Lo, then it came to pass,

That Time, to work out her unconscious will,

Once wrought the mind which she had groped to fill,

And she beheld herself as in a glass.

The world of men, unrolled before our sight,

Showed like a map, where stream and waterfall,

And village-cradling vale and cloud-capped height

Stand faithfully recorded, great and small,

For Shakespeare was, and at his touch with light

Impartial as the sun's, revealed the All.

"Shakespeare Sonnets, VII." *Poetical Works*. Ed. Arthur Symons. 1900, p. 443.

ALFRED, LORD TENNYSON, **BEFORE** 1892
(1809-1892)

THERE are three repartees in Shakespeare which always bring tears to my eyes from their simplicity.

One is in *King Lear*, when Lear says to Cordelia, "So young and so untender," and Cordelia lovingly answers, "So young, my lord, and true." And in *The Winter's Tale*, when Florizel takes Perdita's hand to lead her to the dance, and says, "So turtles pair that never mean to part," and the little Perdita answers, giving her hand to Florizel, "I'll swear for 'em." And in *Cymbeline*, when Imogen in tender rebuke says to her husband:

"Why did you throw your wedded lady from you?

Think that you are upon a rock; and now,

Throw me again!"

and Posthumus does not ask forgiveness, but answers, kissing her:

"Hang there like fruit, my soul,

Till the tree die."

Life and Works of Alfred, Lord Tennyson. Ed. Hallam, Lord Tennyson. 1898, vol. iv. pp. 39 *et seq.*

See also *ib.*, pp. 39-43.

SIDNEY LEE, 1899
(*b.* 1859)

SHAKESPEARE'S mind, as Hazlitt suggested, contained within itself the germs of all faculty and feeling. He knew intuitively how every faculty and feeling would develop in any conceivable change of fortune. Men and women—good or bad, old or young, wise or foolish, merry or sad, rich or poor—yielded their secrets to him, and his genius enabled him to give being in his pages to all the shapes of humanity that present themselves on the highway of life. Each of his characters gives voice to thought or passion with an individuality and a naturalness that rouse in the intelligent playgoer and reader the illusion that they are overhearing men and women speak unpremeditatingly among themselves, rather than that they are reading written speeches or hearing written speeches recited. The more closely the words are studied, the completer the illusion grows. Creatures of the imagination—fairies, ghosts, witches—are delineated with a like potency, and the reader or spectator feels instinctively that these supernatural entities could not speak, feel, or act otherwise than Shakespeare represents them. The creative power of poetry was never manifested to such effect as in the corporeal semblances in which Shakespeare clad the spirits of the air.

So mighty a faculty sets at nought the common limitations of nationality, and in every quarter of the globe to which civilised life has penetrated, Shakespeare's power is recognised. All the world over, language is applied to his creations that ordinarily applies to beings of flesh and blood. Hamlet and Othello, Lear and Macbeth, Falstaff and Shylock, Brutus and Romeo, Ariel and Caliban are studied in almost every civilised tongue as if they were historic personalities, and the chief of the impressive phrases that fall from their lips are rooted in the speech of civilised humanity. To Shakespeare the intellect of the world, speaking in divers accents, applies with one accord his own words: "How noble in reason! how infinite in faculty! in apprehension how like a god!"

Life of William Shakespeare. 1899, chap. xxi.

PART II
"GOOD SENTENCES"

Good sentences.

Merchant of Venice, I. ii. 11.

Brief, short, quick, snap.

Merry Wives, IV. v. 2.

In the quick forge and working-house of thought.

Henry V. V. prol. 23.

A good swift simile.

Taming of the Shrew, V. ii. 54.

"GOOD SENTENCES"

> SHAKESPEARE, we must be silent in thy praise,
> 'Cause our encomions will but blast thy bays,
> Which envy could not, that thou didst so well,
> Let thine own histories prove thy chronicle.

ANONYMOUS. Epig. 25. *Witts Recreations*. 1640, printed 1639.

> TO-DAY we bring old gather'd herbs, 'tis true,
> But such as in sweet Shakespeare's garden grew.
> And all his plants immortal you esteem,

Your mouths are never out of taste with him.

JOHN CROWNE (d. 1703?). Prologue to *Henry the Sixth, the First Part*. Adapted from Shakespeare's *1 Henry VI*. 1681. Sig. A2.

SHAKESPEARE (whom you and every playhouse bill

Style the divine, the matchless, what you will)

For gain, not glory, wing'd his roving flight,

And grew immortal in his own despite.

ALEXANDER POPE (1688-1744). *Imitations of Horace*. Bk. II. ch. i. ll. 69-72. 1737.

THRICE happy! could we catch great Shakespeare's art,

To trace the deep recesses of the heart;

His simple plain sublime, to which is given

To strike the soul with darted flame from heaven.

JAMES THOMSON (1700-1748). Prologue to *Tancred and Sigismundâ*. 1745. Sig. A4.

LET others seek a monumental fame,

And leave for one short age a pompous name;

Thou dost not e'en this little tomb require,

Shakespeare can only with the world expire.

Epitaph on a Tombstone of Shakespeare. *Gentleman's Magazine*. June 1767, vol. xxvii. p. 324.

SHAKESPEARE came out of Nature's hand like Pallas out of Jove's head, at full growth and mature.

GEORGE COLMAN (1733-1794), before 1767.

George Colman, who advocated the theory that Shakespeare had some classic learning, commenting in the Appendix to the second edition of his translation of the comedies of Terence (1768) on Richard Farmer's *Essay on the Learning of Shakespeare* (1767), which maintains that Shakespeare got his knowledge of the ancients from translations, says: "Mr. Farmer closes these general testimonies of Shakespeare's having been only indebted to Nature, by saying, 'He came out of her hand, *as some one else expresses it*, like Pallas out of Jove's head, at full growth and mature.' It is whimsical enough, that this *some one else*, whose expression is here quoted to countenance the general notion of Shakespeare's want of literature, should be no other than myself. Mr. Farmer does not choose to mention where he met with this expression of *some one else*; and *some one else* does not choose to mention where he dropped it." Colman's "Appendix" was printed in the "Variorum" editions of Shakespeare, and that of 1785 gave an anonymous note, stating that Young "in his *Conjectures on Original Composition* (vol. v. p. 100, ed. 1773) has the following sentence: 'An adult genius comes out of Nature's hands, as Pallas out of Jove's head, at full growth and mature.' Shakespeare's genius was of this kind." Young's *Conjectures* appeared in 1759, so perhaps Colman borrowed, though, as he says (*Prose on Several Occasions*, 1787, ii. p. 186), "The thought is obvious, and might, without improbability, occur to different writers." At any rate, his form of the thought is better than Young's, so he has here been given the credit for it.

TO mark her Shakespeare's worth, and Britain's love,

Let Pope design, and Burlington approve:

Superfluous care! when distant times shall view

This tomb grown old—his works shall still be new.

RICHARD GRAVES (1715-1804). "On erecting a Monument to Shakespeare under the direction of Mr. Pope and Lord Burlington." *Euphrosyne*, 1776.

This refers to the monument erected by public subscription in Westminster Abbey in 1741. The design was by William Kent, and the statue of Shakespeare, which was part of it, was executed by Peter Scheemachers.

OUR modern tragedies, hundreds of them do not contain a good line; nor are they a jot the better, because Shakespeare, who was superior to all mankind, wrote some whole plays that are as bad as any of our present writers'.

HORACE WALPOLE (1717-1797). Letter to Sir Horace Mann, Oct. 8, 1778. *Letters*. Ed. Peter Cunningham, 1858, vol. vii. p. 135.

WRITE like Shakespeare, and laugh at the critics.

DANIEL WEBB (1719?-1798). *Literary Amusements*, 1787, p. 22.

SHAKESPEARE, . . .

Lord of the mighty spell: around him press

Spirits and fairy forms. He, ruling wide

His visionary world, bids terror fill

The shivering breast, or softer pity thrill

E'en to the inmost heart.

W. L. BOWLES (1762-1850). "Monody on the Death of Dr. Warton," 1801. *Poems*, 1803, vol. ii. pp. 141-2.

IS there no bard of heavenly power possess'd,

To thrill, to rouse, to animate the breast?

Like Shakespeare o'er the sacred mind to sway,

And call each wayward passion to obey?

F. D. HEMANS (1793-1835). "England and Spain," 1807.

OUR love of Shakespeare, therefore, is not a *monomania* or solitary and unaccountable infatuation; but is merely the natural love which all men bear to those forms of excellence that are accommodated to their peculiar character, temperament, and situation; and which will always return, and assert its power over their affections, long after authority has lost its reverence, fashions been antiquated, and artificial tastes passed away.

FRANCIS LORD JEFFREY (1773-1850). *Edinburgh Review*, Aug. 1811, vol. xviii. p. 285.

SHAKESPEARE had the inward clothing of a fine mind; the outward covering of solid reading, of critical observation, and the richest eloquence; and compared with these, what are the trappings of the schools?

GEORGE DYER (1755-1841). "The Relation of Poetry to the Arts and Sciences," in *The Reflector*, 1811. Reprinted in *Poetics*, 1812, ii. p. 19.

SHAKESPEARE has been accused of profaneness. I for my part have acquired from perusal of him, a habit of looking into my own heart, and am confident that Shakespeare is an author of all others the most calculated to make his readers better as well as wiser.

S. T. COLERIDGE (1772-1834). "Outline of an introductory Lecture on Shakespeare," 1812.

LET no man blame his son for learning history from Shakespeare.

Id. Seven Lectures on Shakespeare and Milton. Ed. J. P. Collier, p. 19.

THE greatest genius that, perhaps, human nature has yet produced, our *myriad-minded*[232:1] Shakespeare.

Id. Biographia Literaria, 1817, chap. xv.

THE great, ever-living, dead man.

Ibid.

HUMANITY'S divinest son,

That sprightliest, gravest, wisest, kindest one—

Shakespeare.

LEIGH HUNT (1784-1859). *Thoughts of the Avon on 28 Sept. 1817.*

HIS plays alone are properly expressions of the passions, not descriptions of them. His characters are real beings of flesh and blood; they speak like men, not like authors.

WILLIAM HAZLITT (1778-1830). "On Shakespeare and Milton," *Lectures on the English Poets*, 1818, p. 98.

IN trying to recollect any other author, one sometimes stumbles, in case of failure, on a word as good. In Shakespeare, any other word but the true one, is sure to be wrong.[234:1]

Ibid., p. 108.

SHAKESPEARE was the least of a coxcomb of any one that ever lived, and much of a gentleman.

Ibid., p. 111.

> . . . DIVINEST Shakespeare's might
>
> Fills Avon and the world with light,
>
> Like omniscient power which he
>
> Imaged 'mid mortality.

P. B. SHELLEY (1792-1822). "Lines written among the Euganean Hills," October 1818.

SHAKESPEARE led a life of allegory: his works are the comments on it.

JOHN KEATS (1795-1821). Letter to George and Georgiana Keats, 18 Feb. 1819.

IF we wish to know the force of human genius, we should read Shakespeare. If we wish to see the insignificance of human learning, we may study his commentators.

WILLIAM HAZLITT (1778-1830). *Table Talk*, 1821, vol. i. p. 177.

> . . . SHAKESPEARE, who in our hearts for himself hath erected an empire
>
> Not to be shaken by time, nor e'er by another divided.

ROBERT SOUTHEY (1774-1843). *A Vision of Judgment*, 1821, ix. ll. 17, 18.

I LOOK upon him to be the worst of models, though the most extraordinary of writers.

LORD BYRON (1788-1824). Letter to Murray, 14 July 1821. Moore's *Life of Byron*.

SCHILLER has the material sublime: to produce an effect, he sets you a whole town on fire, and throws infants with their mothers into the flames, or locks up a father in an old tower. But Shakespeare drops a handkerchief, and the same or greater effects follow.

S. T. COLERIDGE (1772-1834). *Table Talk*, 29 Dec. 1822.

AN immortal man,—

Nature's chief darling, and illustrious mate,

Destined to foil old Death's oblivious plan,

And shine untarnish'd by the fogs of Fate,

Time's famous rival till the final date!

THOMAS HOOD (1799-1845). *The Plea of the Midsummer Fairies*, cv. 1827, p. 53.

WHO knows or can figure what the Man Shakespeare was, by the first, by the twentieth, perusal of his works? He is a Voice coming to us from the Land of Melody: his old brick dwelling-place, in the mere earthly burgh of Stratford-on-Avon, offers us the most inexplicable enigma.

THOMAS CARLYLE (1795-1881). *Critical and Miscellaneous Essays*, "Goethe." Reprinted from *Foreign Review*, No. 3, 1828.

STUDENTS of poetry admire Shakespeare in their tenth year; but go on admiring him more and more, understanding him more and more, till their threescore-and-tenth.

Ibid.

No one can understand Shakespeare's superiority fully until he has ascertained, by comparison, all that which he possessed in common with several other great dramatists of his age, and has then calculated the surplus which is entirely Shakespeare's own.

S. T. COLERIDGE (1772-1834). *Table Talk*, 12 May 1830.

> HIS was the wizard spell,
>
> The spirit to enchain:
>
> His grasp o'er nature fell,
>
> Creation own'd his reign.

"Poetical Portraits" by A Modern Pythagorean in *Blackwood's Edinburgh Magazine*, vol. xxvii. 1830, p. 632.

It is not too much to say, that the great plays of Shakespeare would lose less by being deprived of all the passages which are commonly called the fine passages, than those passages lose by being read separately from the play. This is, perhaps, the highest praise which can be given to a dramatist.

LORD MACAULAY (1800-1859). *Edinburgh Review*, June 1831, vol. liii. pp. 567-8.

I BELIEVE Shakespeare was not a whit more intelligible in his own day than he is now to an educated man, except for a few local allusions of no consequence. And I said, he is of no age—nor, I may add, of any religion, or party, or profession. The body and substance of his works came out of the unfathomable depths of his own oceanic mind: his observation and reading, which were considerable, supplied him with the drapery of his figures.

S. T. COLERIDGE (1772-1834). *Table Talk*, 15 March 1834.

I WOULD be willing to live only as long as Shakespeare were the mirror to Nature.

Id., Letters, etc., 1836, i. 196.

THAN Shakespeare and Petrarch pray who are more living?

Whose words more delight us? whose touches more *touch*?

LEIGH HUNT (1784-1859). "Blue-stocking Revels; or, the Feast of the Violets." Canto III. *Monthly Repository*, 1837.

IN the gravest sense it may be affirmed of Shakespeare, that he is among the modern luxuries of life.

T. DE QUINCEY (1785-1859). "Shakespeare," *Encyclopædia Britannica*, 7th ed., 1842. Written 1838.

PRODUCE us from any drama of Shakespeare one of those leading passages that all men have by heart, and show us any eminent defect in the very sinews of the thought. It is impossible; defects there may be, but they will always be found irrelevant to the main central thought, or to its expression.

Id. "Pope," *Encyclopædia Britannica*, 7th ed., 1842. Written 1839.

SHAKESPEARE, a wool-comber, poacher, or whatever else at Stratford in Warwickshire, who happened to write books! The finest human figure, as I apprehend, that Nature has hitherto seen fit to make of our widely diffused Teutonic clay. Saxon, Norman, Celt or Sarmat, I find no human soul so beautiful, these fifteen hundred known years;—our supreme modern European man.

THOMAS CARLYLE (1795-1881). "Geschichte der Teutschen Sippschaft," translated by Carlyle in *Chartism*, 1839. *Critical and Miscellaneous Essays*.

IT is to be doubted whether even Shakespeare could have told a story like Homer, owing to that incessant activity and superfœtation of thought, a little less of which might be occasionally desired even in his plays;—if it were possible, once possessing anything of his, to wish it away.

LEIGH HUNT (1784-1859). "What is Poetry?" *Imagination and Fancy*, 1844. Ed. A. S. Cook, 1893, p. 65.

NOW, literature, philosophy, and thought are Shakespearised. His mind is the horizon beyond which, at present, we do not see.

R. W. EMERSON (1803-1882). "Representative Men." *Shakespeare; or the Poet,* 1844.

SHAKESPEARE, on whose forehead climb

The crowns o' the world: O eyes sublime,

With tears and laughter for all time!

E. B. BROWNING (1809-1861). *A Vision of Poets,* 1844.

A RIB of Shakespeare would have made a Milton: the same portion of Milton, all poets born ever since.

W. S. LANDOR (1775-1846). "Imaginary Conversations." *Works,* 1846, ii. p. 74.

IN poetry there is but one supreme,

Tho' there are many angels round his throne,

Mighty, and beauteous, while his face is hid.

Id. "On Shakespeare." "Poems and Epigrams." *Works,* 1846.

A LONG list can be cited of passages in Shakespeare, which have been solemnly denounced by many eminent men (all blockheads) as ridiculous: and if a man *does* find a passage in a tragedy that displeases him, it is sure to seem ludicrous: witness the indecent exposures of themselves made by Voltaire, La Harpe, and many billions beside of bilious people.

T. DE QUINCEY (1785-1859). "Schlosser's Literary History." *Tait's Magazine,* Sept., Oct., 1847.

A THOUSAND poets pried at life,

And only one amid the strife

Rose to be Shakespeare.

R. BROWNING (1812-1889). *Christmas Eve and Christmas Day*, xvi., 1850.

WHEN I began to give myself up to the profession of a poet for life, I was impressed with a conviction, that there were four English poets whom I must have continually before me as examples—Chaucer, Shakespeare, Spenser, and Milton. These I must study, and equal *if I could*; and I need not think of the rest.

WILLIAM WORDSWORTH (1770-1850). *Memoirs*. By Christopher Wordsworth, 1851, vol. ii. p. 470.

I CANNOT account for Shakespeare's low estimate of his own writings, except from the sublimity, the superhumanity of his genius. They were infinitely below his conception of what they might have been, and ought to have been.

Ibid.

. . . MATCHLESS Shakespeare, who, undaunted, took

From Nature's shrinking hand her secret book,

And page by page the wondrous tome explored.

D. M. MOIR (1798-1851), before 1851. "Stanzas on an Infant." *Poetical Works*, 1852, vol. ii. p. 50.

SHAKESPEARE'S glowing soul,

Where mightiness and meekness met.

Ibid., p. 341, "Hymn to the Moon."

KIND Shakespeare, our recording angel.

T. L. BEDDOES (1803-1849). "Lines written in Switzerland." *Poems*, 1851, vol. i. p. 215.

KINDER all earth hath grown since genial Shakespeare sung!

EDWARD BULWER, LORD LYTTON (1805-1873). "The Souls of Books," i. l. 21. *Works*, 1853, vol. iii. p. 282.

SHAKESPEARE . . .

. . . Wise and true,

Bright as the noon-tide, clear as morning dew,

And wholesome in the spirit and the form.

CHARLES MACKAY (1814-1899). "Mist." *Under Green Leaves*, 1857.

I CARE not how Shakespeare is acted: with him the thought suffices.

ABRAHAM LINCOLN (1809-1865), *c.* 1860.

I AM always happy to meet persons who perceive the transcendent superiority of Shakespeare over all other writers.

R. W. EMERSON (1803-1882). "Culture." *Conduct of Life*, 1860.

WE may consider Shakespeare, as an ancient mythologist would have done, as "enskied" among "the invulnerable clouds," where no shaft, even of envy, can assail him. From this elevation we may safely predict that he never can be plucked.

CARDINAL WISEMAN (1802-1856). *William Shakespeare*, 1865, p. 28.

TO say truth, what I most of all admire are the traces he shows of a talent that could have turned the *History of England* into a kind of *Iliad*, almost perhaps into a kind of *Bible*.

THOMAS CARLYLE (1795-1881). "Shooting Niagara: and After?" *Macmillan's Magazine*, August, 1867.

SHAKESPEARE! loveliest of souls,

Peerless in radiance, in joy.

MATTHEW ARNOLD (1822-1888). "Heine's Grave." *New Poems*, 1867, p. 198.

IF Shakespeare did not know the ancients, I think they were at least as unlucky in not knowing him.

J. R. LOWELL (1819-1891). *Among my Books*, 1870, p. 190.

SHAKESPEARE recognised both our human imperfections and our human greatness. . . . A woman is dearer to Shakespeare than an angel; a man is better than a god.

EDWARD DOWDEN (*b*. 1843). *Shakespeare: His Mind and Art*, 1875, p. 346.

SHAKESPEARE frequently has lines and passages in a strain quite false, and which are entirely unworthy of him. But one can imagine his smiling if one could meet him in the Elysian Fields and tell him so; smiling and replying that he knew it perfectly well himself, and what did it matter?

MATTHEW ARNOLD (1822-1888). "Preface to Poems of Wordsworth," 1879. *Essays in Criticism*, 2nd ser., p. 135.

ALL Castaly flowed crystalline

In gentle Shakespeare's modulated breath.

D. G. ROSSETTI (1828-1882). "On certain Elizabethan Revivals." *Recollections of D. G. Rossetti*. By T. Hall Caine, 1882, p. 256.

CONCEPTION, fundamental brain work, that is what makes the difference in all art. Work your metal as much as you like, but first take care that it is gold, and worth working. A Shakespearean sonnet is better than the most perfect in form, because Shakespeare wrote it.

Ibid., p. 249.

I CLOSE your Marlowe's page, my Shakespeare's ope,

How welcome—after gong and cymbal's din—

The continuity, the long slow slope

And vast curves of the gradual violin!

WILLIAM WATSON (*b*. 1858). *Epigrams of Art, Life, and Nature*, 1884, vii.

SHAKESPEARE illustrates every phase and variety of humour: a complete analysis of Shakespeare's humour would make a system of psychology.

G. MOULTON (*b*. 1849). *Shakespeare as a Dramatic Artist*, 1893, p. 285.

FROM Shakespeare, no doubt, the world may learn, and has learnt, much; yet he professed so little to be a teacher, that he has often been represented as almost without personal opinions, as a mere undisturbed mirror, in which all Nature reflects herself. Something like a century passed before it was perceived that his works deserved to be in a serious sense studied.

J. R. SEELEY (1834-1895). *Goethe reviewed after Sixty Years*, 1894, p. 98.

SHAKESPEARE and Chaucer throw off, at noble work, the lower part of their natures as they would a rough dress.

JOHN RUSKIN (1819-1900). *Fors Clavigera*. Letter XXXIV., 1896, ii. 235.

PART III
"ROUND ABOUT"

What's here? A scroll; and written round about?

Let's see.

Titus Andronicus, IV. ii. 19.

With his steerage shall your thoughts grow on.

Pericles, IV. iv. 19.

Falstaff. Of what quality was your love, then?

Ford. Like a fair house built on another man's ground.

Merry Wives, II. ii. 223.

"ROUND ABOUT"

MARGARET CAVENDISH, DUCHESS OF NEWCASTLE, 1664 (1624?-1674)

REMEMBER, when we were very young maids, one day we were discoursing about lovers, and we did enjoin each other to confess who professed to love us, and whom we loved, and I confessed I was in love with three dead men, which were dead long before my time, the one was Cæsar, for his valour, the second Ovid, for his wit, and the third our countryman Shakespeare, for his comical and tragical humour; but soon after we both married two worthy men, and I will leave you to your own husband, for you best know what he is. As for my husband, I know him to have the valour of Cæsar, the fancy and wit of Ovid, and the tragical, especially comical art of Shakespeare, in truth, he is as far beyond Shakespeare for comical humour, as Shakespeare is beyond an ordinary poet in that way.

Letter CLXII. *CCXI Sociable Letters written by the Lady Marchioness of Newcastle*, 1664. Letters CXXIII. and CLXII.

JOSEPH ADDISON, 1711
(1672-1719)

SOME years ago I was at the tragedy of "Macbeth," and unfortunately placed myself under a woman of quality, that is since dead; who, as I found by the noise she made, was newly returned from France. A little before the rising of the curtain, she broke out into a loud soliloquy, "When will the dear witches enter?" and immediately upon their first appearance, asked a lady that sat three boxes from her, on her right hand, if those witches were not charming creatures. A little later, as Betterton was in one of the finest speeches of the play, she shook her fan at another lady, who sat as far on her left hand, and told her in a whisper that might be heard all over the pit, "We must not expect to see Balloon to-night." Not long after, calling out to a young baronet by his name, who sat three seats before me, she asked him whether Macbeth's wife was still alive; and before he could give an answer, fell a-talking of the ghost of Banquo. She had by this time formed a little audience to herself, and fixed the attention of all about her. But as I had a mind to hear the play, I got out of the sphere of her impertinence, and planted myself in one of the remotest corners of the pit.

The Spectator, No. 45, 21 April 1711.

HENRY FIELDING, 1743
(1707-1754)

I THEN observed Shakespeare standing between Betterton and Booth, and deciding a difference between these two great actors concerning the placing an accent in one of his lines: this was disputed on both sides with a warmth which surprised me in Elysium, till I discovered by intuition that every soul retained its principal characteristic, being, indeed, its very essence. The line was that celebrated one in *Othello*—

Put out the light, and then put out the light,

according to Betterton. Mr. Booth contended to have it thus:—

Put out the light, and then put out *the* light.

I could not help offering my conjecture on this occasion, and suggested it might perhaps be—

Put out the light, and then put out *thy* light.

Another hinted a reading very sophisticated in my opinion—

Put out the light, and then put out *thee*, light.

Making light to be the vocative case. Another would have altered the last word, and read—

Put out thy light, and then put out thy *sight*.

But Betterton said, if the text was to be disturbed, he saw no reason why a word might not be changed as well as a letter, and instead of "put out thy light," you may read "put out thy eyes." At last it was agreed on all sides to refer the matter to the decision of Shakespeare himself, who delivered his sentiments as follows: "Faith, gentlemen, it is so long since I wrote the line, I have forgot my meaning. This I know, could I have dreamt so much nonsense would have been talked and writ about it, I would have blotted it out of my works; for I am sure, if any of these be my meaning, it doth me very little honour."

He was then interrogated concerning some other ambiguous passages in his works; but he declined any satisfactory answer; saying, if Mr. Theobald had not writ about it sufficiently, there were three or four more new editions of his plays coming out, which he hoped would satisfy every one: concluding, "I marvel nothing so much as that men will gird themselves at discovering obscure beauties in an author. Certes the greatest and most pregnant beauties are ever the plainest and most evidently striking; and when two meanings of a passage can in the least balance our judgments which to prefer, I hold it matter of unquestionable certainty that neither of them is worth a farthing."

From his works our conversation turned on his monument; upon which Shakespeare, shaking his sides, and addressing himself to Milton, cried out, "On my word, brother Milton, they have brought a noble set of poets together; they would have been hanged erst have convened such a company at their tables when alive." "True, brother," answered Milton, "unless we had been as incapable of eating then as we are now."

"A Journey from this World to the Next," Chapter viii. *Miscellanies*, 1743.

THOMAS EDWARDS, 1747
(1699-1757)

CANON I. A Professed Critic has a right to declare that his Author wrote whatever He thinks he ought to have written, with as much positiveness as if he had been at his elbow.

CANON II. He has a right to alter any passage which He does not understand.

CANON III. These alterations He may make in spite of the exactness of measure.

CANON IV. Where He does not like an expression, and yet cannot mend it, He may abuse his Author for it.

CANON V. Or He may condemn it as a foolish interpolation.

CANON VI. As every Author is to be corrected into all possible perfection, the Professed Critic is the sole judge; He may alter any word or phrase, which does not want amendment, or which *will do*, provided He can think of anything which He imagines *will do better*.

CANON VII. He may find out obsolete words, or coin new ones, and put them in the place of such as He does not like, or does not understand.

CANON VIII. He may prove a reading or support an explanation by any sort of reasons, no matter whether good or bad.

CANON IX. He may interpret his Author so as to make him mean directly contrary to what he says.

CANON X. He should not allow any poetical licences, which He does not understand.

CANON XI. He may make foolish amendments or explanations, and refute them, only to enhance the value of his critical skill.

CANON XII. He may find out a bawdy or immoral meaning in his Author where there does not appear to be any hint that way.

CANON XIII. He need not attend to the low accuracy of orthography, or pointing; but may ridicule such trivial criticisms in others.

CANON XIV. Yet, when He pleases to condescend to such work, He may value himself upon it; and not only restore lost puns, but point out such quaintnesses where, perhaps, the Author never thought of them.

CANON XV. He may explain a difficult passage by words absolutely unintelligible.

CANON XVI. He may contradict himself for the sake of showing his critical skill on both sides of the question.

CANON XVII. It will be necessary for the Professed Critic to have by him a good number of pedantic and abusive expressions, to throw about upon proper occasions.

CANON XVIII. He may explain his Author, or any former Editor of him, by supplying such words, or pieces of words, or marks, as He thinks fit for that purpose.

CANON XIX. He may use the very same reasons for confirming his own observations, which he has disallowed in his adversary.

CANON XX. As the design of writing notes is not so much to explain the Author's meaning as to display the Critic's knowledge, it may be proper, to show his universal learning, that He minutely point out from whence every metaphor and allusion is taken.

CANON XXI. It will be proper, in order to show his wit, especially if the Critic be a married man, to take every opportunity of sneering at the fair sex.

CANON XXII. He may mis-quote himself, or anybody else, in order to make an occasion of writing notes, when he cannot otherwise find one.

CANON XXIII. The Professed Critic, in order to furnish his quota to the bookseller, may write notes of nothing; that is to say, notes which either explain things which do not want explanation, or such as do not explain matters at all, but merely fill up so much paper.

CANON XXIV. He may dispense with truth, in order to give the world a higher idea of his parts, or the value of his work.

The Canons of Criticism, first published as a *Supplement to Mr. Warburton's Edition of Shakespear. Collected from Notes in that Celebrated Work, and proper to be bound up with it.* By the OTHER GENTLEMAN of *Lincoln's* Inn.

Warburton's edition also elicited *An Attempte to Rescue that Auncient English Poet and Play-Wrighte, Maister Willaume Shakespere, from the many Errores faulsely charged on him by Certaine New-fangled Wittes, by a Gentleman formerly of Greys-Inn.* 1749. This small treatise dealt with *The Tempest* in a spirit of genuine zeal, but with less controversial ability than was displayed by the "Other Gentleman."

MARK AKENSIDE, 1749
(1721-1770)

"The Remonstrance of Shakespeare: supposed to have been spoken at the Theatre Royal, while the French comedians were acting by subscription. 1749."

IF, yet regardful of your native land,

Old Shakespeare's tongue you deign to understand,

Lo, from the blissful bowers where Heaven rewards

Instructive sages and unblemish'd bards,

I come, the ancient founder of the stage,

Intent to learn, in this discerning age,

What form of wit your fancies have embrac'd,

And whither tends your elegance of taste,

That thus at length our homely toils you spurn,

That thus to foreign scenes you proudly turn,

That from my brow the laurel wreath you claim

To crown the rivals of your country's fame.

What though the footsteps of my devious Muse

The measur'd walks of Grecian art refuse?

Or though the frankness of my hardy style

Mock the nice touches of the critic's file?

Yet, what my age and climate held to view,

Impartial I survey'd, and fearless drew.

And say, ye skilful in the human heart,

Who know to prize a poet's noblest part,

What age, what clime, could e'er an ampler field

For lofty thought, for daring fancy, yield?

I saw this England break the shameful bands

Forg'd for the souls of men by sacred hands:

I saw each groaning realm her aid implore;

Her sons the heroes of each warlike shore;

Her naval standard (the dire Spaniard's bane)

Obey'd through all the circuit of the main.

Then too great Commerce, for a late-found world,

Against your coast her eager sails unfurl'd:

New hopes, new passions, thence to bosom fir'd;

New plans, new arts, the genius thence inspir'd;

Thence every scene, which private fortune knows,

In stronger life, with bolder spirit, rose.

Disgrac'd I this full prospect which I drew?

My colours languid, or my strokes untrue?

Have not your sages, warriors, swains, and kings

Confess'd the living draught of men and things?

What other bard in any clime appears

Alike the master of your smiles and tears?

Yet have I deigned your audience to entice

With wretched bribes to luxury and vice?

Or have my various scenes a purpose known

Which freedom, virtue, glory, might not own?

Such from the first was my dramatic plan,

It should be yours to crown what I began:

And now that England spurns her Gothic chain,

And equal laws and social science reign,

I thought, Now surely shall my zealous eyes

View nobler bards and juster critics rise,

Intent with learned labour to refine

The copious ore of Albion's native mine,

Our stately Muse more graceful airs to teach,

And form her tongue to more attractive speech,

Till rival nations listen at her feet,

And own her polish'd as they own'd her great.

But do you thus my favourite hopes fulfil?

Is France at last the standard of your skill?

Alas for you! that so betray a mind

Of art unconscious and to beauty blind.
Say; does her language your ambition raise,
Her barren, trivial, unharmonious phrase,
Which fetters eloquence to scantiest bounds,
And maims the cadence of poetic sounds?
Say; does your humble admiration choose
The gentle prattle of her Comic Muse,
While wits, plain-dealers, fops, and fools appear,
Charg'd to say nought but what the king may hear?
Or rather melt your sympathising hearts,
Won by her tragic scene's romantic arts,
Where old and young declaim on soft desire,
And heroes never, but for love, expire?
No. Though the charms of novelty, awhile,
Perhaps too fondly win your thoughtless smile,
Yet not for you design'd indulgent fate
The modes or manners of the Bourbon state.
And ill your minds my partial judgment reads,
And many an augury my soul misleads,
If the fair maids of yonder blooming train
To their light courtship would an audience deign,
Or those chaste matrons a Parisian wife
Choose for the model of domestic life;
Or if one youth of all that generous band,
The strength and splendour of their native land,
Would yield his portion of his country's fame,
And quit old freedom's patrimonial claim,
With lying smiles oppressions pomp to see,
And judge of glory by a king's decree.

O blest at home with justly-envied laws,

O long the chiefs of Europe's general cause,

Whom Heaven hath chosen at each dangerous hour

To check the inroads of barbaric power,

The rights of trampled nations to reclaim,

And guard the social world from bonds and shame;

Oh, let not luxury's fantastic charms

Thus give the lie to your heroic arms:

Nor for the ornaments of life embrace

Dishonest lessons from that vaunting race,

Whom fate's dread laws (for, in eternal fate

Despotic rule was heir to freedom's hate,)

Whom in each warlike, each commercial part,

In civil counsel, and in pleasing art,

The judge of earth predestin'd for your foes,

And made it fame and virtue to oppose.

Odes on Several Subjects. Book II., ode i. *Poetical Works.* Aldine edition, 1835, p. 199.

ROBERT LLOYD, 1751
(1733-1764)

THERE stood an ancient mount, yclept Parnass,

(The fair domain of sacred poesy,)

Which, with fresh odours ever-blooming, was

Besprinkled with the dew of Castaly;

Which now in soothing murmurs whisp'ring glides

Wat'ring with genial waves the fragrant soil,

Now rolls adown the mountain's steepy sides,

Teaching the vales full beauteously to smile,

Dame Nature's handiwork, not form'd by lab'ring toil.

The Muses fair, these peaceful shades among,
With skilful fingers sweep the trembling strings;
The air in silence listens to the song,
And Time forgets to ply his lazy wings;
Pale-visag'd Care, with foul unhallow'd feet,
Attempts the summit of the hill to gain,
Ne can the hag arrive the blissful seat,
Her unavailing strength is spent in vain,
Content sits on the top, and mocks her empty pain.

Oft Phœbus' self left his divine abode,
And here enshrouded in a shady bow'r,
Regardless of his state, laid by the god,
And own'd sweet music's more alluring pow'r.
On either side was plac'd a peerless wight,
Whose merit long had fill'd the trump of Fame;
This, Fancy's darling child, was Spenser hight,
Who pip'd full pleasing on the banks of Tame;
That, no less fam'd than he, and Milton was his name.

.   .   .   .

Next Shakespeare sat, irregularly great,
And in his hand a magic rod did hold,
Which visionary beings did create,
And burn the foulest dross to purest gold:
Whatever spirits rose in earth or air,
Or bad or good, obey his dread command;
To his behests these willingly repair,
Those aw'd by terrors of his magic wand,

The which not all their pow'rs united might withstand.

Beside the bard there stood a beauteous maid,

Whose glittering appearance dimm'd the eyen;

Her thin-wrought vesture various tints display'd,

Fancy her name, ysprong of race divine;

Her mantle wimpled low, her silken hair,

Which loose adown her well-turn'd shoulders stray'd,

She made a net to catch the wanton air,

Whose love-sick breezes all around her play'd,

And seem'd in whispers soft to court the heav'nly maid.

And ever and anon she wav'd in air

A sceptre, fraught with all-creative pow'r:

She wav'd it round: eftsoons there did appear

Spirits and witches, forms unknown before:

Again she lifts her wonder-working wand;

Eftsoons upon the flow'ry plain were seen

The gay inhabitants of Fairy-Land,

And blithe attendants upon Mab their queen

In mystic circles danc'd along th' enchanted green.

On th' other side stood Nature, goddess fair;

A matron seem'd she, and of manners staid;

Beauteous her form, majestic was her air,

In loose attire of purest white array'd:

A potent rod she bore, whose pow'r was such

(As from her darling's works may well be shown,)

That often with its soul-enchanting touch,

She rais'd or joy or caus'd the deep-felt groan,

And each man's passions made subservient to her own.

The Progress of Envy, 1751, Stanzas 2-4 and 7-10.

OLIVER GOLDSMITH, 1765
(1728-1774)

THE character of old Falstaff, even with all his faults, gives me more consolation than the most studied efforts of wisdom: I here behold an agreeable old fellow, forgetting age, and showing me the way to be young at sixty-five. Sure I am well able to be as merry, though not so comical, as he. Is it not in my power to have, though not so much wit, at least as much vivacity?—Age, care, wisdom, reflection, begone!—I give you to the winds. Let's have t'other bottle: here's to the memory of Shakespeare, Falstaff, and all the merry men of Eastcheap.

Such were the reflections that naturally arose while I sat at the Boar's-head tavern, still kept at Eastcheap. Here, by a pleasant fire, in the very room where old Sir John Falstaff cracked his jokes, in the very chair which was sometimes honoured by Prince Henry, and sometimes polluted by his immoral merry companions, I sat and ruminated on the follies of youth; wished to be young again; but was resolved to make the best of life while it lasted, and now and then compared past and present times together.

"A Reverie at the Boar's Head Tavern in Eastcheap." *Collected Essays*, 1765.

GEORGE, LORD LYTTELTON, 1765
(1709-1773)

"Boileau—Pope."

BOILEAU

... THE office of an *editor* was below you, and your mind was unfit for the drudgery it requires. Would anybody think of employing a Raphael to clean an old picture?

POPE

The principal cause of my undertaking that task was zeal for the honour of Shakespeare: and if you knew all his beauties as well as I, you would not wonder at this zeal. No other author had ever so copious, so bold, so *creative* an imagination, with so perfect a knowledge of the passions, the humours, and sentiments of mankind. He painted all characters, from kings down to peasants, with equal truth and equal force. If human nature were destroyed, and no monument were left of it except his works, other beings might know *what man was* from those writings.

BOILEAU

You say he painted all characters, from kings down to peasants, with equal truth and equal force. I cannot deny that he did so; but I wish he had not jumbled those characters together, in the composition of his pictures, as he has frequently done.

POPE

The strange mixture of tragedy, comedy, and farce in the same play, nay, sometimes in the same scene, I acknowledge to be quite inexcusable. But this was the taste of the times when Shakespeare wrote.

BOILEAU

A great genius ought to guide, not servilely follow, the taste of his contemporaries.

POPE

Consider from how thick a darkness of barbarism the genius of Shakespeare broke forth! What were the English, and what (let me ask you) were the French dramatic performances, in the age when he flourished? The advances he made towards the highest perfection both of tragedy and comedy are amazing! In the principal points, in the power of exciting terror and pity, or raising laughter in an audience, none yet has excelled him, and very few have equalled.

BOILEAU

Do you think he was equal in comedy to Moliere?

POPE

In *comic force* I do: but in the fine and delicate strokes of satire, and what is called *genteel comedy*, he was greatly inferior to that admirable writer. There is nothing in him to compare with the *Misanthrope*, the *Ecole des Femmes*, or *Tartuffe*.

BOILEAU

This, Mr. Pope, is a great deal for an Englishman to acknowledge. A veneration for Shakespeare seems to be a part of your national religion, and the only part in which even your men of sense are fanatics.

POPE

He who can read Shakespeare, and be cool enough for all the accuracy of sober criticism, has more of reason than taste.

BOILEAU

I join with you in admiring him as a prodigy of genius, though I find the most shocking absurdities in his plays; absurdities which no critic of my nation can pardon.

POPE

We will be satisfied with your feeling the excellence of his beauties.

Dialogues of the Dead, xiv., 4th edition, 1765. XIV. *Boileau—Pope*, pp. 125-128.

Three editions of *Dialogues of the Dead* were published in 1760. Practically the whole of the passage quoted above appeared for the first time in the fourth edition in 1765.

LAURENCE STERNE, 1768
(1713-1768)

"The Passport—Versailles."

I COULD not conceive why the Count de B * * * had gone so abruptly out of the room, any more than I could conceive why he had put the Shakespeare into his pocket—*Mysteries which must explain themselves, are not worth the loss of time which a conjecture about them takes up*: it was better to read Shakespeare; so, taking up *Much Ado about Nothing*, I transported myself instantly from the chair I sat in to Messina in Sicily, and got so busy with Don Pedro and Benedick and Beatrice, that I thought not of Versailles, the Count, or the Passport.

Sweet pliability of man's spirit, that can at once surrender itself to illusions, which cheat expectation and sorrow of their wearied moments!—long, long since had you numbered out my days, had I not trod so great a part of them upon this enchanted ground: when my way is too rough for my feet, or too steep for my strength, I get off it, to some smooth velvet path which fancy has scattered over with rosebuds of delights; and, having taken a few turns in it, come back strengthened and refreshed—When evils press sore upon me, and there is no retreat from them in this world, then I take a new course—I leave it—and as I have a clearer idea of the Elysian fields than I have of heaven, I force myself, like Æneas, into them—I see him meet the pensive shade of his forsaken Dido—and wish to recognise it—I see the injured spirit wave her head, and turn off silent from the author of her miseries and dishonours—I lose the feelings for myself in hers—and in those affections which were wont to make me mourn for her when I was at school.

Surely this is not walking in a vain shadow—nor does man disquiet himself in vain *by it*—he oftener does so in trusting the issue of his commotions to reason only—I can safely say for myself, I was never able to conquer any one single bad sensation in my heart so decisively, as by beating up as fast as I could some kindly and gentle sensation, to fight it upon its own ground.

When I had got to the end of the third act, the Count de B * * * entered with my passport in his hand. M. Le Duc de C * * *, said the Count, is as good a prophet, I dare say, as he is a statesman—*Un homme qui rit*, said the Duke, *ne sera jamais dangereux.* Had it been for any one but the King's jester, added the Count, I could not have got it these two hours—*Pardonnez moi*, M. Le Compte, said I—I am not the King's jester—But you are Yorick?—Yes—*Et vous plaisantez?*—I answered, Indeed I did jest—but was not paid for it—it was entirely at my own expense.

We have no jester at court, M. Le Compte, said I—the last we had was in the licentious reign of Charles II.—since which time our manners have been so gradually refining, that our court at present is so full of patriots, who wish for *nothing* but the honours and wealth of their country—and our ladies are all so chaste, so spotless, so good, so devout—there is nothing for a jester to make a jest of—

Voila un persiflage! cried the Count.

Yorick's Sentimental Journey through France and Italy, etc., 1768, vol. ii.

ANONYMOUS, 1769

"*The Dramatic Race. A Catch. By a Lover of the Turf.*"

> CLEAR, clear the course—make room—make room, I say!
>
> Now they are off, and *Jonson* makes the play.
>
> I'll bet the odds—done, sir, with you, and you;
>
> SHAKESPEARE keeps near him—and he'll win it too:
>
> Here's even money—done for a hundred, done—
>
> Now, *Jonson!* now or never—he has won.
>
> I'll take my oath, that SHAKESPEARE won the prize,—
>
> Damme! whoever says he lost it, lies.

Shakespeare's Garland. Being a Collection of New Songs, Ballads, Roundelays, Catches, Glees, Comic Serenatas, etc., performed at the Jubilee at Stratford-upon-Avon, 1769, p. 16.

ISAAC BICKERSTAFF, 1769
(d. 1812?)

"Queen Mab. A Cantata."

RECITATIVE

NOT long ago, 'tis said, a proclamation

Was sent abroad through all the Fairy nation;

Mab to her loving subjects—A decree,

At Shakespeare's tomb to hold a Jubilee.

ACCOMPANIED

The night was come, and now on Avon's side

The pigmy race was seen,

Attended by their queen,

On chafers some, and some on crickets ride.

The queen appear'd from far,

Mounted in a nut-shell car;

Six painted lady-birds the carriage drew:

And now the cavalcade,

In order due array'd,

March'd first

Where erst

The sacred Mulb'ry grew,

And there their homage paid.

Next they sought the holy ground,

And while

A thousand glow-worm torches glimmer'd round;

Thus Good Fellow, the herald of his fame,

Did from the alabaster height proclaim

The poet's titles and his style.

AIR

SHAKESPEARE, heaven's most favour'd creature,

Truest copier of Nature,

First of the Parnassian train;

Chiefest fav'rite of the Muses,

Which soe'er the poet chooses,

Blest alike in ev'ry strain.

Life's great censor, and inspector,

Fancy's treasurer, wit's director,

Artless, to the shame of art;

Master of the various passions,

Leader of all inclinations,

Sov'reign of the human heart.

RECITATIVE

Then did the queen an acorn take,

Fill'd with morn and ev'ning dew,

Brush'd from ev'ry fragrant brake

That round the lawns of Stratford grew.

ACCOMPANIED

"And thus," said she, "libation do I make

To our friend and father's shade:

'Twas Shakespeare that the Fairies made;

And men shall give us honour for his sake."

AIR

O happy bard, whose potent skill

Can give existence where it will!

Let giant wisdom strive to chase

From man's belief the Fairy race;

Religion stern our pow'r reject,

Philosophy our tales neglect,

Only trusting what 'tis seeing;

Combat us howe'er they list,

In thy scenes we shall exist,

Sure as if Nature gave us being.

Shakespeare's Garland. Being a Collection of New Songs, Ballads, Roundelays, Catches, Glees, Comic Serenatas, etc., performed at the Jubilee at Stratford-upon-Avon, 1769, p. 21.

This piece was set to music by Dibdin.

ANONYMOUS, 1778

"Shakespeare's Bedside, or his Doctors enumerated."

> OLD Shakespeare was sick;—for a doctor he sent;—
> But 'twas long before any one came:
> Yet at length his assistance Nic Rowe did present,
> Sure all men have heard of his name.
>
> As he found that the Poet had tumbled his bed,
> He smooth'd it as well as he could;
> He gave him an anodyne, comb'd out his head,
> But did his complaint little good.
>
> Doctor Pope to incision at once did proceed,
> And the Bard for the simples he cut;

For his regular practice was always to bleed,
Ere the fees in his pocket he put.

Next Theobald advanc'd, who at best was a quack,
And dealt but in old women's stuff;
Yet he caus'd the Physician of Twick'nam to pack,
And the patient grew cheerful enough.

Next Hanmer, who fees ne'er descended to crave,
In gloves lily-white did advance;
To the Poet the gentlest of purges he gave,
And, for exercise, taught him to dance.

One Warburton then, though allied to the Church,
Produc'd his alternative stores;
But his med'cines the case so oft left in the lurch,
That Edwards kick'd him out of doors.

Next Johnson arriv'd to the patient's relief,
And ten years he had him in hand;
But, tir'd of his task, 'tis the general belief,
He left him before he could stand.

Now Capell drew near,—not a Quaker more prim,—
And numbered each hair on his pate;
By styptics, call'd stops, he contracted each limb,
And crippled for ever his gait.

From Gopsall then strutted a formal old goose,
And he'd cure him by inches, he swore;
But when the poor Poet had taken one dose,
He vow'd he would swallow no more.

But Johnson, determin'd to save him, or kill,

A second prescription display'd;

And, that none might find fault with his drop or his pill,

Fresh doctors he call'd to his aid.

First Steevens came loaded with black-letter books,

Of fame more desirous than pelf;

Such reading, observers might read in his looks,

As no one e'er read but himself.

Then Warner, by Plautus and Glossary known,

And Hawkins, historian of sound;

Then Warton and Collins together came on,

For Greek and Potatoes renown'd.

With songs on his pontificalibus pinn'd,

Next Percy the great did appear;

And Farmer, who twice in a pamphlet had sinn'd,

Brought up his empirical rear.

"The cooks the more numerous, the worse is the broth,"

Says a proverb I well can believe;

And yet to condemn them untried I am loth,

So at present shall laugh in my sleeve.

Gentleman's Magazine, 1787, vol. lvii. ii. 912. *Muses' Mirror*, 1778, i. 90.

"Edwards,"—the author of *Canons of Criticism*, see p. 281.

"Capell . . . numbered each hair on his pate,"—Edward Capell (see p. 107), of whom Dr. Johnson remarked that his abilities "were just sufficient to enable him to select the black hairs from the white for the use of periwig makers." He gave most of his attention to the production of an accurate text, based on a careful collation of the old copies, and he did his work very thoroughly.

"From Gopsall . . . a formal old goose,"—Charles Jennens (1700-1773), who printed some of Shakespeare's tragedies, and brought upon himself the unmerciful ridicule of George Steevens. He lived at Gopsall in Leicestershire.

"Warner,"—Richard Warner (1713?-1775), the botanist and classical scholar. He made extensive collections for an edition and for a glossary of Shakespeare. Neither was published.

"Hawkins,"—Sir John Hawkins (1719-1789), who published *The General History of the Science and Practice of Music*, 1776.

"Warton and Collins,"—Joseph Warton (1722-1800) and William Collins (1721-1759) were school-fellows at Winchester, and life-long friends.

"Percy,"—Bishop Percy of *Percy's Reliques*.

"Farmer,"—Richard Farmer (1735-1797), author of the *Essay on the Learning of Shakespeare*, 1767.

HORACE WALPOLE, EARL OF ORFORD, 1788
(1717-1797)

MY histrionic acquaintance spreads. I supped at Lady Dorothy Hotham's with Mrs. Siddons, have visited and been visited by her, and have seen and liked her much, yes, very much, in the passionate scenes in "Percy"; but I do not admire her in cool declamation, and find her voice very hollow and defective. I asked her in which part she would most wish me to see her? She named Portia in the "Merchant of Venice"; but I begged to be excused. With all my enthusiasm for Shakespeare, it is one of his plays that I like the least. The story of the caskets is silly, and, except the character of Shylock, I see nothing beyond the attainment of a mortal; Euripides, or Racine, or Voltaire might have written all the rest.

Letter to the Countess of Ossory, 15 Jan. 1788. *Letters*, ed. Peter Cunningham, 1859, vol. ix. p. 124.

PAUL WHITEHEAD, 1790
(1710-1774)

> WHILE here to Shakespeare Garrick pays
>
> His tributary thanks and praise;
>
> Invokes the animated stone,
>
> To make the poet's mind his own;
>
> That he each character may trace

With humour, dignity, and grace;
And mark, unerring mark, to men,
The rich creation of his pen:
Preferr'd the prayer—the marble god
Methinks I see, assenting, nod,
And, pointing to his laurell'd brow,
Cry—"Half this wreath to you I owe:
Lost to the stage, and lost to fame;
Murder'd my scenes, scarce known my name;
Sunk in oblivion and disgrace
Among the common scribbling race,
Unnotic'd long thy Shakespeare lay,
To dulness and to time a prey:
But now I rise, I breathe, I live
In you—my representative!
Again the hero's breast I fire,
Again the tender sigh inspire;
Each side, again, with laughter shake,
And teach the villain-heart to quake;
All this, my son! again I do—
I?—No, my son!—'Tis I, and you."
While thus the grateful statue speaks,
A blush o'erspreads the suppliant's cheeks—
"What!—Half this wreath, wit's mighty chief?—
O grant," he cries, "one single leaf;
That far o'erpays his humble merit,
Who's but the organ of thy spirit."
Phoebus the generous contest heard—
When thus the god address'd the bard:

"Here, take this laurel from my brow,

On him your mortal wreath bestow;—

Each matchless, each the palm shall bear,

In heav'n the bard, on earth the play'r."

"Verses dropped in Mr. Garrick's Temple of Shakespeare." *Poems and Miscellaneous Compositions*, 1790.

Garrick had in his garden at Hampton a temple dedicated to Shakespeare, containing a statue of the poet by Roubiliac.

WILLIAM COMBE, 1812
(1741-1823)

"Dr. Syntax in the Pit of Covent Garden Theatre."

CRITIC.—

"Oh, what a *Falstaff!* Oh, how fine!

Oh, 'tis great acting—'tis divine!"

SYNTAX.—

"His acting's great—that I can tell ye;

For all the acting's in his belly."

CRITIC.—

"But, with due def'rence to your joke,

A truer word I never spoke

Than when I say—you've never been

The witness of a finer scene.

Th' admir'd actor whom you see

Plays the fat knight most charmingly:

'Tis in this part he doth excel;

Quin never played it half so well."

Syntax.—

"You ne'er saw Quin the stage adorn:
He acted ere your sire was born,
And critics, sir, who liv'd before you,
Would have disclos'd a different story.
This play I've better acted seen
In country towns where I have been.
I do not hesitate to say—
I'd rather read this very play
By my own parlour fireside,
With my poor judgment for my guide,
Than see the actors of this stage,
Who make me gape at Shakespeare's page.
When I read Falstaff to myself,
I laugh like any merry elf;
While my mind feels a cheering glow
That Shakespeare only can bestow.
The swaggering words in his defence,
Which scarce are wit and yet are sense;
The ribald jest—the quick conceit—
The boast of many a braggart feat;
The half-grave questions and replies
In his high-wrought soliloquies;
The dubious thought—the pleasant prate,
Which give no time to love or hate,
In such succession do they flow,
From no to yea—from yea to no,
Have not been to my mind convey'd
By this pretender to his trade.

The smile sarcastic, and the leer

That tells the laughing mock'ry near;

The warning look, that ere 'tis spoke

Aptly forbodes the coming joke;

The air so solemn, yet so sly,

Shap'd to conceal the ready lie;

The eyes, with some shrewd meaning bright,

I surely have not seen to-night:

Again, I must beg leave to tell ye,

'Tis nought of Falstaff but his belly."

CRITIC.—

"All this is fine—and may be true;

But with such truths I've nought to do.

I'm sure, sir, I shall say aright,

When I report the great delight

Th' enraptur'd audience feel to-night;

It is indeed, with no small sorrow,

I cannot your opinions borrow

To fill the columns of to-morrow.

My light critique will be preferr'd,

The public always takes my word;

Nay, the loud plaudits heard around

Must all your far-fetch'd thoughts confound:

I truly wonder when I see

You do not laugh as well as me."

SYNTAX.—

"My muscles other ways are drawn:

I cannot laugh, sir,—while I yawn."

CRITIC.—

"But you will own the scenes are fine?"

SYNTAX.—

"Whate'er the acting, they're divine,
And fit for any pantomime.
Of this it is that I complain;
These are the tricks which I disdain:
The painter's art the play commends;
On gaudy show success depends:
The clothes are made in just design;
They are well character'd and fine.
The actors now, I think, Heav'n bless 'em,
Must learn their art from those who dress 'em;
But give me actors, give me plays,
On which I could with rapture gaze,
Tho' coats and scenes were made of baise:
For if the scene were highly wrought;
If actors acted as they ought;
You would not then be pleased to see
This heavy mass of frippery.
Hear Horace, sir, who wrote of plays
In Ancient Rome's Augustan days:—
'Tanto cum strepitu ludi spectantur, et artes,
Divitiæque peregrinæ: quibus oblitus actor
Cum stetit in scena, concurrit dextera lævæ.
Dixit adhuc aliquid? Nil sane. Quid placet ergo?
Lana Tarentino violas imitata veneno.'"

CRITIC.—

"Your pardon, sir, but all around me
There are such noises they confound me:
And though I full attention paid,
I scarcely know a word you said.
To say the truth, I must acknowledge
'Tis long since I have quitted college:
Virgil and Horace are my friends,
I have them at my fingers' ends.
But Grecian lore, I blush to own,
Is wholly to my mind unknown.
I therefore must your meaning seek:
Oblige me, sir, translate your Greek.
But see, the farce is now begun,
And you must listen to the fun,
It sure has robb'd you of your bile;
For now, methinks, you deign to smile."

SYNTAX.—

"The thing is droll, and aptly bent
To raise a vulgar merriment:
But Merry-Andrews, seen as such,
Have often made me laugh as much.
An actor does but play the fool
When he forsakes old Shakespeare's rule,
And lets his own foul nonsense out,
To please th' ill-judging rabble rout:
But when he *swears*, to furnish laughter,
The beadle's whip should follow after."

The Tour of Dr. Syntax in search of the Picturesque. 1812, Canto XXIV. ll. 173 *sq.*

Tanto cum strepitu, etc., Horace, *Epistles*, II. i. 203-7.

CHARLES LAMB, 1826.
(1775-1834)

YOUR fair critic in the coach reminds me of a Scotchman who assured me that he did not see much in Shakespeare. I replied, I dare say *not*. He felt the equivoke, lookd awkward, and reddish, but soon returnd to the attack, by saying that he thought Burns was as good as Shakespeare: I said that I had no doubt he was—to a *Scotchman*. We exchangd no more words that day.

Letter to J. B. Dibdin, June 30, 1826. *Works of Charles and Mary Lamb*. Ed. E. V. Lucas. 1903-4. Vol. vii.

NATHANIEL HAWTHORNE, 1845
(1804-1864)

THE human race had now reached a stage of progress so far beyond what the wisest and wittiest men of former ages had ever dreamed of, that it would have been a manifest absurdity to allow the earth to be any longer encumbered with their poor achievements in the literary line. Accordingly, a thorough and searching investigation had swept the booksellers' shops, hawkers' stands, public and private libraries, and even the little bookshelf by the country fireside, and had brought the world's entire mass of printed paper, bound or in sheets, to swell the already mountain-bulk of our illustrious bonfire. Thick, heavy folios, containing the labours of lexicographers, commentators, and encyclopedists, were flung in, and, falling among the embers with a leaden thump, smouldered away to ashes, like rotten wood. The small, richly-gilt French tomes of the last age, with the hundred volumes of Voltaire among them, went off in a brilliant shower of sparkles, and little jets of flame; while the current literature of the same nation burnt red and blue, and threw an infernal light over the visages of the spectators, converting them all to the aspect of parti-coloured fiends. A collection of German stories emitted a scent of brimstone. The English standard authors made excellent fuel, generally exhibiting the properties of sound oak logs. Milton's works, in particular, sent up a powerful blaze, gradually reddening into a coal, which promised to endure longer than almost any other material of the pile. From Shakespeare there gushed a flame of such marvellous splendour, that men shaded their eyes as against the sun's meridian glory; nor even when the works of his own elucidators were flung upon him, did he cease to flash forth a dazzling radiance beneath the ponderous heap. It is my belief that he is still blazing as fervidly as ever.

"Could a poet but light a lamp at that glorious flame," remarked I, "he might then consume the midnight oil to some good purpose."

"That is the very thing which modern poets have been too apt to do, or at least to attempt," answered a critic. "The chief benefit to be expected from this conflagration of past literature undoubtedly is, that writers will henceforth be compelled to light their lamps at the sun or stars."

Mosses from an Old Manse. "Earth's Holocaust," ii. 146-7.

WALTER SAVAGE LANDOR, 1846
(1775-1864)

"Shakespeare and Bacon."

SOUTHEY.—In so wide and untrodden a creation as that of Shakespeare's, can we wonder or complain that sometimes we are bewildered and entangled in the exuberance of fertility? Dry-brained men upon the continent, the trifling wits of the theatre, accurate however and expert calculators, tell us that his beauties are balanced by his faults. The poetical opposition, puffing for popularity, cry cheerily against them, *his faults are balanced by his beauties*; when, in reality, all the faults that ever were committed in poetry would be but as air to earth, if we could weigh them against one single thought or image, such as almost every scene exhibits in every drama of this unrivalled genius. Do you hear me with patience?

PORSON.—With more; although at Cambridge we rather discourse on Bacon, for we know him better. He was immeasurably a less wise man than Shakespeare, and not a wiser writer: for he knew his fellow-man only as he saw him in the street and in the Court, which indeed is but a dirtier street and a narrower; Shakespeare, who also knew him there, knew him everywhere else, both as he was and as he might be.

SOUTHEY.—There is as great a difference between Shakespeare and Bacon as between an American forest and a London timber-yard. In the timber-yard the materials are sawed and squared and set across; in the forest we have the natural form of the tree, all its growth, all its branches, all its leaves, all the mosses that grow about it, all the birds and insects that inhabit it; now deep shadows absorbing the whole wilderness; now bright bursting glades, with exuberant grass and flower and fruitage; now untroubled skies; now terrific thunderstorms; everywhere multiformity, everywhere immensity.

"Southey and Porson." *Imaginary Conversations. Works,* 1846, i. pp. 12-13.

This is from the enlarged edition of the *Imaginary Conversations*. It does not appear in the original Southey-Porson "Conversation" published in 1824.

WILLIAM SCHWENCK GILBERT, 1868
An Unfortunate Likeness
(b. 1836)

I'VE painted Shakespeare all my life,
"An Infant" (even then at "play"!)
"A boy" with stage-ambition rife,
Then "married to Ann Hathaway."

"The bard's first ticket night" (or "ben."),
His "First appearance on the stage,"
His "Call before the curtain"—then
"Rejoicings when he came of age."

The bard play-writing in his room,
The bard a humble lawyer's clerk,
The bard a lawyer—parson—groom—
The bard deer-stealing, after dark.

The bard a tradesman—and a Jew—
The bard a botanist—a beak—
The bard a skilled musician too—
A sheriff and a surgeon eke!

Yet critics say (a friendly stock)
That, though it's evident I try,
Yet even *I* can barely mock
The glimmer of his wondrous eye!

One morning as a work I framed,
There passed a person, walking hard:

"My gracious goodness," I exclaimed,
"How very like my dear old bard!

"Oh what a model he would make!"
I rushed outside—impulsive me!—
"Forgive the liberty I take,
But you're so very"—"Stop!" said he.

"You needn't waste your breath or time,—
I know what you are going to say,—
That you're an artist, and that I'm
Remarkably like Shakespeare. Eh?

"You wish that I would sit to you?"
I clasped him madly round the waist,
And breathlessly replied, "I do!"
"All right," said he, "but please make haste."

I led him by his hallowed sleeve,
And worked away at him apace,
I painted him till dewy eve,—
There never was a nobler face!

"Oh sir," I said, "a fortune grand
Is yours, by dint of merest chance,—
To sport *his* brow at second hand,
To wear *his* cast-off countenance!

"To rub *his* eyes whene'er they ache—
To wear *his* baldness ere you're old—
To clean *his* teeth when you awake—
To blow *his* nose when you've a cold!"

His eyeballs glistened in his eyes—

I sat and watched and smoked my pipe;
"Bravo!" I said, "I recognise
The phrensy of your prototype!"

His scanty hair he wildly tore:
"That's right," said I, "it shows your breed."
He danced—he stamped—he wildly swore—
"Bless me, that's very fine indeed!"

"Sir," said the grand Shakespearean boy
(Continuing to blaze away),
"You think my face a source of joy;
That shows you know not what you say.

"Forgive these yells and cellar-flaps:
I'm always thrown in some such state
When on his face well-meaning chaps
This wretched man congratulate.

"For oh! this face—this pointed chin—
This nose—this brow—these eyeballs too,
Have always been the origin
Of all the woes I ever knew!

"If to the play my way I find,
To see a grand Shakespearean piece,
I have no rest, no ease of mind,
Until the author's puppets cease.

"Men nudge each other—thus—and say,
'This certainly is Shakespeare's son,'
And merry wags (of course in play)
Cry 'Author,' when the piece is done.

"In church the people stare at me,
Their soul the sermon never binds;
I catch them looking round to see,
And thoughts of Shakespeare fill their minds.

"And sculptors, fraught with cunning wile,
Who find it difficult to crown
A bust with Brown's insipid smile
Or Tomkins's unmannered frown,

"Yet boldly make my face their own,
When (oh, presumption!) they require
To animate a paving-stone
With Shakespeare's intellectual fire.

"At parties where young ladies gaze,
And I attempt to speak my joy,
'Hush, pray,' some lovely creature says,
'The fond illusion don't destroy!'

"Whene'er I speak, my soul is wrung
With these or some such whisperings:
''Tis pity that a Shakespeare's tongue
Should say such un-Shakespearean things!'

"I should not thus be criticised
Had I a face of common wont:
Don't envy me—now, be advised!"
And, now I think of it, I don't!

Reprinted from *Fun*, 14 Nov. 1868.

"The bard a lawyer"—

"Go with me to a notary: seal me there
Your single bond."

Merchant of Venice, I. iii.
"Parson"—

"And there shall she at friar Laurence' cell
Be shriv'd, and married."

Romeo and Juliet, II. iv.
"Groom"—

"And give their fasting horses provender."

Henry V., IV. ii.
"A tradesman"—

"Let us, like merchants, show our foulest wares."

Troilus and Cressida, I. iii.
"A Jew"—

"Then must the Jew be merciful."

Merchant of Venice, IV. i.
"A botanist"—

"The spring, the summer,
The chiding autumn, angry winter, change
Their wonted liveries."

Midsummer Night's Dream, II. ii.
"A beak"—
"In the county of Gloster, justice of the peace, and coram."
Merry Wives of Windsor, I. i.
"A skilled musician"—

"What lusty trumpet thus doth summon us?"

King John, V. ii.

"A sheriff"—

"And I'll provide his executioner."

II Henry VI., III. i.

"A surgeon"—

"The lioness had torn some flesh away,
Which all this while had bled."

As You Like It, IV. iii.

W. S. GILBERT.

OLIVER WENDELL HOLMES, 1872
(1809-1894)

I WONDER if anything like this ever happened:—

Author writing,—

"To be, or not to be: that is the question:
Whether 'tis nobl—"

"William, shall we have pudding to-day, or flapjacks?"

"Flapjacks an it please thee, Anne, or a pudding for that matter; or what thou wilt, good woman, so thou come not betwixt me and my thought."

Exit Mistress Anne, with strongly accented closing of the door, and murmurs to the effect: "Ay, marry, 'tis well for thee to talk as if thou hadst no stomach to fill. We poor wives must swink for our masters, while they sit in their arm-chairs, growing as great in the girth through laziness as that ill-mannered old fat man, William, hath writ of in his books of players' stuff. One had as well meddle with a porkpen, which hath thorns all over him, as try to deal with William when his eyes be rolling in that mad way."

William—writing once more—after an exclamation in strong English of the older pattern,—

"Whether 'tis nobler—nobler—nobler—

To do what? O these women! these women! to have puddings or flapjacks! Oh!

"Whether 'tis nobler—in the mind—to suffer

The slings—and arrows—of—

Oh! Oh! these women! I'll e'en step over to the parson's, and have a cup of sack with his reverence, for methinks Master Hamlet hath forgot that which was just now on his lips to speak."

The Poet at the Breakfast-Table, 1872, pp. 10-11.

THEODORE WATTS-DUNTON, 1897

"Shakespeare's Friend speaks."

> TO sing the nation's song, or do the deed
>
> That crowns with richer light the motherland,
>
> Or lend her strength of arm in hour of need,
>
> When fangs of foes shine fierce on every hand,
>
> Is joy to him whose joy is working well—
>
> Is goal and guerdon too, though never fame
>
> Should find a thrill of music in his name;
>
> Yea, goal and guerdon too, though Scorn should aim
>
> Her arrows at his soul's high citadel.
>
> But if the fates withhold the joy from me
>
> To do the deed that widens England's day,
>
> Or join that song of Freedom's jubilee
>
> Begun when England started on her way—
>
> Withhold from me the hero's glorious power
>
> To strike with song or sword for her, the mother,
>
> And give that sacred guerdon to another,

Him will I hail as my more noble brother—

Him will I love for his diviner dower.

Enough for me who have our Shakespeare's love

To see a poet win the poet's goal,

For Will is he; enough and far above

All other prizes to make rich my soul.

"Christmas at the Mermaid." *The Coming of Love, and Other Poems*, 1898 .

JUDGE WILLIS, 1902
(b. 1835)

"Examination of Edward Blount, one of the printers and publishers of the Shakespeare folio of 1623."

DID you never hear that Shakespeare the actor, whom you knew, had nothing to do with the pieces published under his name?

I never did.

Did you never hear that the name "Shakespeare," that is, with the "e" after the "k," was assumed to cover and conceal the writings of a very great, distinguished man?

I never did.

Would you be surprised to hear that Lord Bacon—

The reporter says that as soon as this word escaped from Counsel's lips, the whole Court was convulsed with laughter, in which the jury joined.

To save appearances, the learned Judge retired into his private room, as he said, in order to fetch his copy of "Venus and Adonis." His laughter was heard in the hall.

"We noticed," says the reporter, "that Mr. Jonson never smiled. He seemed deeply moved, and exclaimed, 'What next? And next?'"

On the return of the Judge, the laughter had not quite subsided, and the usher cried "Order, Order."

The Judge, on again taking his seat, said to the Counsel for the defence, "I am sorry, sir, your question should have been so received, but you must remember the spectators are human, and that the jury and myself are not free from infirmity. We are, however, quite impartial."

The Counsel resumed.

Now that this indecent laughter is over, tell me, sir, do you not know that Lord Bacon was the author of the plays contained in the folio volume?

I do not know it, and never until now have I heard a doubt cast upon the authorship of Shakespeare.

Did you never have any communication from Lord Bacon in respect of the publishing the folio volume?

Never. I never received a paper of any kind from him, nor did I communicate any portion of the manuscript to him.

Did not Mr. Benjamin Jonson bring you the manuscripts, or some of them, from which you printed?

"My lord, my lord!" said Jonson.

"Pray be quiet, Mr. Jonson, you will have your turn directly," said the Judge.

He did not, nor did he touch any sheet of them. As I have told you, I never communicated with him until I spoke to him about writing some lines for the portrait.

Did not Mr. Jonson write the Dedication or Preface?

He wrote neither. Heminge and Condell wrote the Dedication, and the Address to the Readers they composed in consultation with myself.

Did you not receive money from some one in order to induce you to print the folio?

I did not. I looked to the sale, and the sale only, to recoup myself and my co-adventurers.

Re-examined.—I myself never touched the manuscripts, nor added a line to them. After they were in my possession, Heminge and Condell never, to my knowledge, altered the manuscripts, nor did any one else.

I could, if necessary, have written a Dedication and the Address to the Readers. I wrote a work entitled "A Hospital for Incurable Fools." I hope some day such hospital will be founded.

The Shakespeare-Bacon Controversy; A Report of The Trial of an Issue in Westminster Hall, 20 June 1627. Read in the Inner Temple Hall, Thursday, May the 29th, 1902, by William Willis, Treasurer of the Honourable Society of the Inner Temple, pp. 15-16.

This extract is taken from an account of an imaginary suit in connection with the administration of Shakespeare's estate, to determine whether the testator was the author of the plays published under the name of William Shakespeare in the folio volume of 1623.

The *Dictionary of National Biography* states that Edward Blount (*fl.* 1588-1632), the stationer, has been credited on doubtful grounds with the authorship of the very curious *Hospitall of Incvrable Fooles: Erected in English, as neer the first Italian Modell and platforme as the vnskilful hand of an ignorant Architect could deuise. Printed by Edm. Bollifant for Edward Blount*, 1600.

TO MY VERY GOOD FRIEND, MR. WILLIAM SHAKESPEARE

It's not because I know that you

Are really what the World has found you,

That I collect and tell anew

The tributes that have gathered round you.

Not moved to tread the lofty ways

Of those great souls who turned their powers,

As duty-bounden, to your praise,

Weave I this little wreath of flowers.

You have, I know, a "myriad mind,"

A "honey tongue" to tell a story;

You left poor "panting Time" behind,

(See Johnson) in the race for glory—

'Tis true. But when all's said and done,

With thought and rhetoric impassioned,

You've been, and are, a Friend to one

Whose mind is not supremely fashioned.

FOOTNOTES:

[vii:1] This volume bore the title, *Studies of Shakspere: introductory volume, containing A History of Opinion on the Writings of Shakspere; with the Chronology of his Plays.* The book in this form seems now to be difficult of access. No copy of it is in the British Museum Library. I acquired a copy for a few pence many years ago.

[5:1] I can myself add nothing but suggestions of possible borrowings from Shakespearean diction. In the poem, *The Court Burlesqu'd*, printed in Samuel Butler's *Remains*, the lines—

> "This, by a rat behind the curtain
>
> Has been o'erheard, some say for certain,"

may be reminiscent of the scene in *Hamlet* in which Polonius is killed; and in Quarles' *Argalus and Parthenia*, the expression "to gild perfection," which occurs in the 21st line of the first book, seems to echo the passage in *King John*, "to gild refined gold, to paint the lily," etc.

[10:1] In 1756.

[19:1] Johnson several times expresses himself in a like spirit in his *Rambler*:

"It may be doubtful whether from all his successors more maxims of theoretical knowledge, or more rules of practical prudence, can be collected than he alone has given to his country."—*Works*, v. 131.

"He that has read Shakespeare with attention will, perhaps, find little new in the crowded world."—*Ib.* 434.

"Let him that is yet unacquainted with the powers of Shakespeare, and who desires to feel the highest pleasure that the drama can give, read every play, from the first scene to the last, with utter negligence of all his commentators. When his fancy is on the wing, let it not stoop at correction or explanation."—*Ib.* 152.

[26:1] A word may be said here of the eighteenth century anthologists. Collections of poems were numerous. That by Dodsley, with its supplement prepared by Pearch, contains nothing by Shakespeare, nor indeed does Nichols' collection, which claimed to include no poem that had been printed in the volumes issued by Dodsley or Pearch. A collection by Thomas Tomkins, entitled *Poems on Various Subjects: selected to enforce the Practice of Virtue, and with a View to comprise in One Volume the Beauties of*

English Poetry (1787), goes no farther back than Milton; and the well-known anthology, *Select Beauties of Ancient English Poetry*, with remarks by Henry Headley, contains such names as Drayton, Warner, Drummond, Raleigh, Surrey, Carew, Wyat, and Browne, but Shakespeare finds no place. He does not, in fact, enter regularly collections of this kind until the beginning of the nineteenth century—the period of "Elegant Extracts." But he is quoted frequently enough in Edward Bysshe's *Art of English Poetry* (1724); and John Bowle, in his *Miscellaneous Pieces of Ancient English Poetry* (1765), selects from *King John*.

[28:1] *Literary Remains* (1836), vol. ii. p. 63.

[185:1] The last line in the earlier version—that printed in the *Academy*—has "tailor's" for "Starveling's." Rossetti made the alteration from fear of offending sensitive members of the tailoring profession.

[232:1] Coleridge says that he borrowed this phrase from a Greek monk, who applied it to a Patriarch of Constantinople.

[234:1] "These remarks," Hazlitt adds, "are strictly applicable only to the impassioned parts of Shakespeare's language, which flowed from the warmth and originality of his imagination, and were his own. The language used for prose conversation and ordinary business is sometimes technical, and involved in the affectation of the time."